Blue Jasmine

Kashmira Sheth

Hyperion Paperbacks
for Children
New York

First Hyperion Paperbacks edition, 2006

This book is set in Barret Normal.

3 5 7 9 10 8 6 4 2

Printed in the United States of America

Library of Congress Cataloging-in-Publication Data on file.

ISBN 0-7868-1855-7 (tr.)
ISBN 0-7868-5565-7 (pbk.)

Visit www.hyperionbooksforchildren.com

In loving memory of my pappa,
Arvindbhai A. Trivedi

MY HEARTFELT THANKS:

To my mother, Bharatiben,
for her blessings and her steadfast faith in my ability.

To my precious daughters, Rupa and Neha,
for all their hugs, encouragement, and countless readings
of this manuscript.

To my husband, Rajan,
for his love and support.

To my uncle and aunt, Rohit and Susan Trivedi,
for making Iowa my second home.

To Marjorie Melby for all the editing, comments,
and especially for her friendship.

To Donna Bray, Arianne Lewin, and Emily van Beek, my editors
and supporters at Hyperion, for their insight, enthusiasm, and
guidance.

To all of my family and friends for their interest,
inspiration, and excitement for this book.

THE TRIVEDI FAMILY

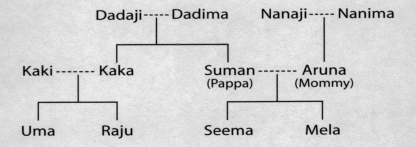

Dadaji ----- Dadima   Nanaji ----- Nanima

Kaki ------- Kaka   Suman -------- Aruna
                      (Pappa)   (Mommy)

Uma   Raju   Seema   Mela

---- marriage
—— children

ONE

"So what if this summer is cooler than last, Seema? Last summer you were not leaving us. Last summer our family was not breaking up. I wish this year and this summer had never come. I hate this year!" Raju said. He swung his face away and spat. Without looking back, he sprinted home.

I stood near the acacia tree growing at the edge of an abandoned lot and watched Raju's back as the dust rising from his shoes covered my white blouse and my beige pinafore. I didn't worry about my clothes. School was over, and I would never wear this uniform again. But Raju's anger worried me. I glanced at the acacia. It was brown and bare except for the thorns. It looked like a starved stray dog baring its teeth. I started walking home.

Raju was my cousin, and I wanted to tell him that

everything would be fine—but how could I? Today was the last day of fifth grade, and after summer vacation when sixth grade started, he would be walking to school by himself. For the first time, I wouldn't be going with him. I would be in America.

Only a few months earlier, when the mango trees were jeweled with purplish-green leaves and milky-white blossoms, a letter came that changed everything. At that time, Mommy and my four-year-old sister, Mela, had gone to see Mommy's parents, my Nanaji and Nanima. The letter was from Dr. Davis, and Pappa was excited. "Seema," he said to me, "Dr. Davis wants me to go to Iowa City to work with him."

Pappa was a microbiologist. He loved his work, and some days when he got busy doing experiments in his laboratory, he forgot to eat lunch. On these days my grandmother made one of his favorite dishes for dinner. I never could understand how Pappa could forget his lunch while working with tiny bugs that he could only see under a microscope. When I was eight, Pappa had gone to Iowa City for three months during the summer to work with Dr. Davis, and I had missed him. I didn't want him to go away again this summer.

"How long will you be gone this time?" I asked.

"We'll all go this time," he said, stroking my long hair.

"All of us?"

"I mean, Mommy, Mela, you, and I," he said.

"What about the rest of the family?" I asked. In our family, besides Mommy, Pappa, Mela, and me, there was my grandfather, Dadaji; my grandmother, Dadima; Pappa's older brother, my *kaka*; his wife, my *kaki*; and their two children, my cousins Uma and Raju.

"We can't all go," Pappa said.

"But you just said, 'We'll all go this time.'"

"I meant the four of us, Seema."

From that day on, the four of us, Pappa, Mommy, Mela, and I, broke off from our family the way a lump of ice breaks off from a whole snow cone. In some ways the lump is still the same as it was on the snow cone, but somehow, after it breaks off, it's different. It melts away too fast and it doesn't taste as good as the whole cone does.

When Pappa told me that Dr. Davis wanted him to work in his laboratory, I asked, "You mean, we would . . . we would go and live in Iowa, and I would go to school there?"

"Yes! Would you like that?"

"I . . . I don't know."

He looked at me. He was as excited as Mela when Dadaji lifted her up and bounced her on his knees.

"Does Raju know yet?" I asked.

"Kaka and Kaki are telling Uma and Raju right now."

That night I wondered why they hadn't told all of us at the same time. Why had Kaka and Kaki told Uma and Raju, and why had Pappa told me?

When I went to bed, I wondered how I could leave the rest of my family and go to America. We all lived in the same house, ate in the same kitchen. Raju and I went to school together and were in the same class. Raju was my cousin, but he was as much my brother as he was Uma's brother. He was my best friend.

I missed Mommy that night. Pappa was so happy about going to America that I didn't want to talk to him about my fears, but I wanted Mommy to hold me tight and tell me that without the rest of the family we would be fine. That we would go to the new country and make new friends. Pappa had called Mommy and told her about our going to America, and I wondered if Mommy herself was as scared about the move as I was.

That night my sleep didn't flow like a stream, but came in spurts, like the water that spewed from our faucet, on and off, in the heat of the summer. The next morning I was tired and groggy.

At breakfast Uma was quiet and kept stirring her milk with a spoon, while Raju glared at me.

"What is it?" I asked Raju.

"What is what?" he snapped back.

"Why are you staring at me?"

"Am I?" he said.

"Yes, why?"

"I don't know. Do you?"

"Why do you keep answering me with a question?" I asked.

"Why do you keep asking me questions?" he answered.

Uma glanced at me. Her eyes were red. And then it occurred to me that last night Kaka and Kaki must've told them that we were going to America, and that's why Raju was as sour as stale buttermilk.

It was Saturday, so Raju and I only had school in the morning. In our garden the hibiscus was blooming. The flowers were as red as a parrot's beak, and I wanted to pick one to put in my hair—but I couldn't stop, because Raju kept marching ahead. I tried to hurry, but ended up watching his dark brown hair. It shone with streaks like flame in the sunlight. Our school building was across the grassy field and two streets away. The tall *neem* trees lined the streets, forming a green tent that stopped the wind. As usual, Raju's white shirt was half tucked inside his khaki shorts, half hanging out; but his shoelaces were tied securely. He was the fastest runner in the school and tied his laces very carefully. When we reached school, he slipped away.

For the next few days Raju hardly spoke to me. In class I saw him writing furiously. He covered his writing with his right arm while he wrote with his left hand. I knew it was about our going to America, but he never mentioned it at school or at home.

Slowly, he began talking to me again, but he still wouldn't discuss our leaving for America. For the next few weeks I thought he was fine, until today when I was standing by the acacia tree, and he burst like an overfilled water bottle and ran away.

Why is Raju running away from me? I thought as I reached home. The iron gate was wide open. Inside the front garden, the air was full of the sting of red pepper, and the smell of yellow turmeric, ground cumin, and coriander. Mommy and Kaki were in the back courtyard getting ready to make pickles out of the pieces of green mango that were soaking in a salt-and-turmeric brine. The sight of green mangoes and spices made my mouth water.

"Wash your hands first and then you can have a couple of pieces," Kaki said.

When I came back, Raju had taken three pieces of mango. I took mine and walked out. He followed me, and as I sat on the swing in the front veranda, he sat next to me. The black of the ebony swing and the brass rods that supported it shone brightly in the afternoon sun.

For a while neither one of us spoke.

"You won't be here this year to tie a *rakhi* on me," he said, staring at his wrist.

"I know," I mumbled. I remembered last August, on Rakshabandhan, the special holiday that celebrates the love between brothers and sisters, when I'd made a *rakhi* out of red velvet for Raju. "I'll always make a *rakhi* for you and mail it."

"You won't be here to tie it on me."

"I'll pray to God to keep you safe," I offered.

"It won't be the same. Eating all the good food on Rakshabandhan without you won't be any fun. And I'll have to mail you a gift. I won't be able to see the surprise on your face."

"Raju, you can give me those gifts when I come back."

"Yeah, every ten years! Do you remember what you said to Charu last year when she said that I wasn't your real brother?"

Before I could answer he continued, "I'll remind you. You told her, 'Charu, I'm glad you have two brothers of your own, but I'm happy to have one Raju; I've never felt sad at Rakshabandhan, and I never will.' Now I know Charu was right. If I were your brother and not your cousin, you'd stay here with me. Having a cousin who is like a brother is not the same as having a brother, is it? And when the next Rakshabandhan comes in August, you'll be oceans away from me. You won't be here to tie a *rakhi* on my wrist. Uma will have to do it."

I bit my lip.

"Why do you have to go to America? Why can't you stay here and we can keep going to school together?" Raju pleaded.

"Pappa and Mommy and Mela are going, so I have to go," I said.

"You don't have to! We're all here and you can stay here and go to school with me."

I didn't know what to say. I put one piece of mango in my mouth. It was tart and salty and very refreshing. I sucked on it while I thought. Raju was right. I could stay in Vishanagar, our town in Gujarat, and go to school. There was a girl named Sarla in my class whose mommy and pappa had gone to Canada, but she had stayed behind with her grandparents. One part of me wanted to stay and continue going to school with Raju. Home was like the smell of ripe *kesar* mangoes that made me happy even before I took a bite. If I went to America, everything would be unfamiliar. But another part of me knew that if I stayed behind, I would miss Mommy, Pappa, and Mela too much. The days would pass, but when the sun set, I would be miserable. A slice of me wanted to go to America, to fly away in a big plane and start at a new school and make new friends.

"If you go, nothing will be the same again for me," Raju said.

"I can't stay. I can't stay without Pappa and Mommy."

"What about your school? Everything will be in English. You won't understand what your teachers are saying."

"I know," I said, choking on the mango juice.

"Isn't it better that you stay here?"

"I don't think so."

"Then, go," he said, as he slipped on his sandals and scrambled down the veranda steps.

"Where are you going?" I asked.

"*Jahannam ma!* To hell!" he said.

"Wait!" I shouted.

He didn't look back. "*Jahannam ma!*" I said, and threw the two mango pieces in the flower bed. They hit the *parijat* bush and landed on the gravel. I looked at my hands. They were stained yellow with turmeric. I washed them twice, but the stain wouldn't go away.

That evening, I found out that Raju wasn't the only one who wanted me to stay in India.

During dinner Kaka said to Pappa, "Take Mela to America with you, but leave Seema here with us."

Dadaji agreed, saying, "Suman, I think it is a good idea. The plant flourishes best in its own soil. Mela is too young and needs to be with you, but leave Seema here."

"How can you ask us to leave Seema here?" Pappa wondered.

"Why not? Uma and Seema are the same to me. Both our daughters will be raised the same," Kaka said. I shuddered. I loved Kaka, but his ideas and Pappa's ideas were as different as teeth and tongue. Kaka was as hard as teeth and would never change his opinion, while Pappa was as supple as a tongue and always open to ideas.

"I know Uma and Seema are the same to you, but who knows how long we will stay in America? Seema should come with us," Pappa said. I noticed he hadn't touched his *khichdi*, a mixture of mung beans and rice served with curried potatoes and spinach. It was his favorite food.

"Once you go to America, you will not come back," Kaka warned.

"I . . . we're not sure what we'll do," Pappa said.

"You will stay in America, and if you stay there, then it's even more important to leave Seema here. That way she can grow up in our culture and go to America after high school," Kaka said.

"What kind of talk is this? Seema belongs with her Pappa and Mommy. If they go to America, she goes to America; if they go to Africa, she goes to Africa. If they go for a year, Seema goes for a year; if they go for five years, she goes for five years," Dadima declared as she crumbled a piece of millet bread in a bowl of milk. Lately, for supper, she only ate millet bread soaked in milk.

"Isn't Seema our granddaughter? I say she stays here," Dadaji said.

"I want to go with Pappa and Mommy. I don't want to

stay here." Before I'd realized it, the words sprayed out of my mouth.

"Listen to her! It's important for our children, especially our daughters, to have Indian values. My Uma wouldn't dare talk back to her elders. You've already spoiled Seema, and once you take her to America she will forget our culture and become too independent. I can tell you now that you'll lose a daughter," Kaka said.

"Bhai," Pappa said, "I know you love us and you're concerned about Seema, but she is my daughter and I have to take her with me."

"And you should," Dadima said. "I know Aruna and you would be unhappy if you left Seema behind. Besides, she's growing up and she needs her Mommy more than ever now, and Aruna will need Seema's help in America too."

I glanced at Kaka. He was silent, but I could see that the anger had spread in his body and stiffened it.

Dadaji asked me, "Do you really want to leave us all behind?"

I looked around. All eyes were watching me. Even Mela was quiet. "I . . . I don't know what I want to do. I don't want to leave you, but I . . . want . . . I have to go. I . . . I want to go with Pappa and Mommy," I blurted, trying to curb the rush of tears.

"Then you'd better start packing your bags," Dadima

said, putting her arm around me. She turned to Kaka and added, "There is no reason to discuss this anymore." And to Dadaji she said, "Don't make Seema miserable by asking such questions."

Dadaji nodded a sad smile. I wondered what Mommy and Kaki thought of all this, but they were quiet as rose petals.

That night I kept thinking about our conversation. Even though we slept in the back courtyard, it was warm under the mosquito netting. Once in a while a slight scented breeze carried the smell of jasmine to me. The stars smiled like jewels in the museums: I could see them and admire them, but could never touch them.

Dadima pulled up a chair close to me and began singing a Sanskrit *shloka*, a special prayer. "May everyone be happy, may there be peace for everyone. May good things happen to everyone, may no one suffer any pain."

For a while her singing soothed me, until I realized that once I went to America, Dadima wouldn't be there to ease my sadness.

two

The day after we got our visas from the American Consulate, our neighbors came to say good-bye. My friend Akhil, Raju, Uma, and I sat on the swing and gently rocked back and forth. The heat and humidity of the summer were building, and only the monsoon would break them. But before the monsoon came, I would be in America. I was thinking about how the monsoon would feel in America, when Akhil asked me, "Which state are you going to?"

"Iowa," I replied.

"Iowa? I've never heard of it. It must be Ohi-o."

"No. We're going to Iowa."

"Are you sure you remember the name right? We have many relatives and friends in Ohi-o and I know all about it. I don't think there's a state called Iowa, or I'd have heard about it."

I didn't know what to say. I looked to Raju, but he was gone. Before I panicked, he'd returned with a roll of paper and spread it on the floor. It was a map of America. I hadn't known Raju had a map of America. "Akhil, Seema's going to Iowa. It's right here, west of the Mississippi River," he said, pointing to Iowa. "Ohio is over here. And it's called Ohio, not Ohi-o."

After that Akhil didn't ask me any more questions. When he left I asked Raju, "When did you get the map of America?"

"It's not mine. I borrowed it from Sarla. I wanted to see where you're going."

"When I come back from America I'll bring you your own map," I promised.

He smiled.

For a few days Mommy, Pappa, Mela, and I went to see my other grandparents, Nanaji and Nanima. They lived about eighty miles away in a town called Atul, a quiet place surrounded by mango, coconut, guava, and tamarind trees. Every summer we went there for two weeks, and sometimes Raju and Uma came with us. But this time we were visiting to say good-bye.

At the railway station I wondered when I would see

Nanaji and Nanima again. Nanima had made me a blanket out of her cotton saris and covered it with blue silk satin. Mommy asked me to put it in the bag, but I carried it in my hands. It was as soft as a peacock feather. When we took our seats on the train, Nanaji and Nanima stood on the platform extending their arms through the window. I kissed their hands.

"Seema, take good care of my saris," Nanima said.

"I will," I vowed, clutching my blanket.

I tried not to cry, but when I heard the train's shrill whistle and it began to move in a *chook-chook, chook-chook* rhythm, the tears flooded my cheeks.

When we got home in the evening, Raju said, "One of your friends from school came to see you. Guess who?"

"Anita?" I hadn't seen her since the last day of school.

"Na."

"Nalini? Mita? Urvashi?"

"Na, na, na."

"Who then? Tell me who came."

He waved a small package in his hand and laughed. "Can't you smell who?"

"Mukta?" I said. "Why did she come?" Mukta was in my class, but she was not my friend. The year before we had shared a bench together, but that was because our teacher had assigned our seats. If I had had a choice I would have sat as far away from Mukta as possible. She was not mean and she was a good student, but she smelled like an overflowing gutter in the monsoon. Her uniform stank and her braids stank and even her hands stank.

Raju shrugged his shoulders and gave me the package. As I unwrapped the newspaper, Raju teased, "Be careful now. It might be one of her tiniest pencils, and if it rolls under the bed you'll never find it."

"Raju, quiet," Uma said.

As I opened the package I wondered why Mukta had given me a gift. She was not part of our circle, and Raju barely spoke to her. In class he sat far away from Mukta. I was assigned to sit next to Mukta, but I tried to speak to her as little as possible. The worst was sharing a book with her. I hated her scooting close to me and holding my book with her fingers.

In the package was a soft muslin handkerchief with my name embroidered in one corner. I stared at the water-blue of my name surrounded by sprays of yellow and pink flowers against a white background.

"It's beautiful! Don't you like it?" Uma asked.

"Smell it," I whispered, handing her the handkerchief.

"We can wash it with sandalwood soap and the smell will go away," she said.

When the handkerchief was washed and dried I put it in my suitcase. I thought about visiting Mukta and thanking her, but I didn't. There were always more pressing things to do and more important people to visit.

Two days before we were to leave for America, Mommy and I went to the market. While Mommy was paying the shopkeeper for socks and calamine lotion, I heard someone calling, "Seema, Seema. Over here."

I glanced across the street. For a few seconds I saw only a man carrying a bale of cotton, but when he walked away I spotted a scrawny little girl flapping her arms and calling my name. Mukta? I wondered. She came closer and I saw that I was right. At least in school she wore a uniform like everyone else, but today her clothes were so threadbare that I would've taken her for a beggar. She cut across the sea of shoppers and vendors that lined the street and came to me. "I thought that was you, Seema. When are you leaving?"

"In two days."

"I'm glad I got to see you before you left."

Mommy had paid the shopkeeper by now and stood next to me with a question in her eyes. "Mommy, this is Mukta. We went to school together."

Mommy smiled at Mukta and said, "Seema was thinking about visiting you, but it has been very hectic."

"Please, come now, I live right over there," Mukta said, pointing toward a snack shop.

"We have so much to do, I can't," I said.

"Just for a few minutes, please. Come and meet my family."

I glanced at Mommy, hoping she'd help me avoid visiting Mukta's family, but instead she offered, "Seema, why don't you go with Mukta, and I'll pick up our dry cleaning order down the street." She looked at her watch and added, "It's almost five; I'll meet you here in half an hour."

"In ten minutes?" I asked.

Mommy lifted her eyes in surprise and said, "In twenty minutes."

"I'll bring her back in twenty minutes," Mukta promised, as if she were borrowing a doll to play with. She held her hand out to hold mine, but I kept them safe in my skirt pockets.

"I came to see you last week, but you were away. Raju was there. He told me you went to visit your Nanaji and Nanima. Somehow I thought you'd leave right after visiting them. I'm so glad that I met you today." Mukta jabbered away.

"I wanted to thank you for the embroidered handkerchief you made for me," I said.

"Did you like it? I did all of it myself without any help from anyone. I wanted to make you a set of three, but . . ."

She didn't finish the sentence.

Mukta went up the steps of the shop.

"I thought we were going to your house," I said.

"This is our shop and we live right behind it," she explained. She introduced two men, one sitting behind a frying pan and another kneading dough, as her father and her *kaka*. I'd never seen a snack shop from this close. The frying pan was as large as an elephant's head, and the smoke coming out of it was as gray and thick as elephant skin. My eyes began to sting. I wondered how Mukta's father could sit on a wooden bench all day, every day, and fry savory snacks. It was much warmer inside, and both men wiped sweat away from their faces with a rag every few seconds.

We crossed the shop, and through the rear door we entered Mukta's home. It was one small room. In it, a woman was nursing an infant and another woman was shelling a mound of peas, with the help of a girl about six years old. There were no windows, and the room was dark except for a ray of light that streamed in at an angle through the back door. Dust particles danced in that light. I had seen many poor and homeless people before, but I'd never known anyone so poor. Mukta introduced me to the two women, "Mommy, Kaki, this is my friend Seema. Last year we sat next to each other, but this year she's moving to America."

Mukta's mother stopped shelling peas, stood up, and

spread the sisal rug on the floor, saying, "Come, please sit down." Her voice was sweeter than the tinkling silver bells in the temples.

While Mukta talked I surveyed the room. There was no couch, chair, or even an old *charpoy*, or bed. A kerosene-burning stove hissed with a yellow-blue flame like a wheezing child with a runny nose. The large aluminum pot on the stove was filled with water and was starting to bubble. I wondered what it was for. On the blackened wooden shelves three brass pots and six plates shone brightly. The walls were covered with a layer of grime, and the room reeked with the smell of burned oil, spices, sweat, and . . . something else.

As I was wondering if the unfamiliar smell might be that of infant's urine, a sweet smell of jasmine wafted by. The breeze from the back door had carried the scent, and when I looked out I saw jasmine planted in oil tins covered with double white blooms that were beginning to open up.

Mukta's father poked his head in. He offered fried chickpea noodles and warm potato patties on a newspaper.

"Have some," Mukta's mother urged, but I couldn't pick up a single noodle. The little girl scooted next to me and picked up a noodle. I thought she would eat it. Instead she offered it to me. "Here, eat. It's good," she said.

How could I refuse her?

"Let Mukta and her friend talk. Come and sit by me," Mukta's mother said. The girl didn't move. She took one noodle at a time and handed it to me. I nibbled on each one as long as I could. I don't remember what Mukta and I talked about.

Walking home, Mommy asked, "What's the matter? Are you all right?"

"I'm fine. She's very nice."

"Who's very nice? Mukta?"

"No. Yes. And her mother is very nice too."

"You had a good visit then?" she asked.

"Yes."

We walked silently for a block. "Mommy, I feel terrible," I confessed. "I hated Mukta's stinking clothes, and we made so much fun of her finger-long pencil and old notebooks. Now that I've seen her house, I realize how poor her family is. It's a wonder she even goes to school. I should've . . . I should've . . . I'm so mean."

"No, you're not," she said, squeezing my hand. "As long as you realize your mistake and learn not to make the same mistake again, you can forgive yourself. Aren't you glad that you visited Mukta?"

"Yes. I wonder what will happen to her."

"It's good that she's attending school. Getting an education will help her."

"Do you think she'll go to school for a long time?"

"I don't know," Mommy said. Her brow was tense, and I knew she was concerned about Mukta.

The next morning when I opened my cupboard to pack my suitcase, I saw three school uniforms folded neatly in a stack. "Mommy, do you think we could give these to Mukta?" I asked.

"That's a good idea, but I'm afraid we don't have time to go to Mukta's house."

"Raju, will you take these uniforms to Mukta?" I asked.

"Me? I don't want to go to stinky Mukta's house. Never. Send Zeeno," he said. Zeeno was our servant. I didn't think it was right to send him with my uniforms.

"Mommy, can I quickly go and give these to Mukta?"

"Dadaji is going to the market for vegetables, so go with him and come right back," Mommy said.

When we approached the market I said, "Dadaji, I'll stop and give this package to my friend. You can keep walking and I'll catch up with you in a few minutes."

"Fine. But don't forget your *dadaji* once you start talking to your friend. Come soon."

"I won't forget you," I said, and hurried to Mukta's house.

Mukta was helping in the shop. As soon as she saw me she said, "Come in, come in, Seema."

"I can't. I have to go with my *dadaji*. I came to give

you these," I said, taking a package out of my cotton bag.

"What is it?"

"I have three school uniforms, and I was wondering if you could use them."

"Let me talk to my mommy," she said, and went inside.

Mukta's mother came out and asked, "Seema, how much are the uniforms?"

"They . . . they're . . . no money," I said.

"We can't take them without paying."

"You have to. I mean, please take them. I won't need them in America, and I want Mukta to have them."

"Take them, Mukta," she said, and gave me a smile as bright as a thousand-petal chrysanthemum.

Then she took spicy noodles and lentils and wrapped them in a newspaper and tied them with a string. "Mukta will get much use out of the uniforms, and someday her sister will too," she said, as she handed me the package.

The noodles and lentils had just been fried and the package was still warm. I slipped it in my bag.

"When will you come back from America?" Mukta asked as she walked me back toward the market.

"I don't know."

"I will embroider two handkerchiefs for you, and when you come back they'll be ready."

"You don't have to," I said.

"I know. I want to."

At the end of the street when we'd both said "*Aveje,* come visit" to each other, I felt strange. Someday, I knew I would come back to India, but how would Mukta ever be able to visit me in America?

I caught up with Dadaji right at the entrance of the vegetable market. I realized I didn't know when I'd next be going to the market with Dadaji, and I wanted to soak it all in. Every day, the farmers came from the surrounding farms to sell their produce. Dadaji always bought vegetables from the farmer whose face was parched like the summer earth and whose eyes had a glint of captured sunrays. His white turban, white tunic, and white jodhpurs were all speckled with dust from travel. While weighing our vegetables he sang away, "Eggplants, eggplants, tender eggplants! Eat them with garlic and ginger and keep away from the doctors!"

Then with his trembling hand he gave me a basket of four juice mangoes nestled together. "So many?" I asked.

"Yes, daughter, take it," he pleaded. His voice was heavy with sadness.

I looked at Dadaji for permission. He nodded.

On the way back I asked, "Dadaji, why did the old farmer give me four mangoes? Isn't that a lot to give away?"

"It is," he said. "But you had to take it."

"Why?"

"Two months ago his only granddaughter passed away, and since then he has been a broken man. It mends his heart when he gives away something in her memory."

I wondered if Dadaji was going to be a broken man when Mela and I both left.

As we passed the acacia by the abandoned lot, I remembered Raju's outburst on the last day of school. He had swung his face away and spat before sprinting home. His words still poked me like the thorns of the acacia.

"Why are acacia trees covered in big thorns?" I asked Dadaji.

"To survive, they have to protect themselves from animals, and these thorns do that," he said.

"I think people also grow thorns."

"Who has?"

I told Dadaji that when Raju found out we were leaving for America he didn't speak to me for a long time. I told him what Raju had said to me under the acacia tree and how he'd run away. "Why would he do that, Dadaji? I'll miss him too. I'll miss all of you," I said.

"You will, but don't forget that you're the one making a journey. There's always excitement there. It is harder for the people left behind."

"Yes," I whispered.

When I lay in bed that night the stars looked as if someone had scattered white mustard seeds across a dark iron skillet. I realized how precious it was to have our entire family together. It was the last night of my old life— a life that would soon feel like a dream. I turned to my other side, waiting for my new life to begin far away. One more day hung like a bridge between the two.

"I don't want to come to the airport," I heard Raju say as I came out of the bathroom the next morning. My hair was still dripping water.

"We are all going and so are you," Kaka said.

"I'm not."

Fatak! I heard a slap against Raju's cheek.

Raju turned around and began walking away. "Come back," Kaka ordered.

"I'm not coming back."

"Where are you going?"

"America," he said.

The whole house fell wordless. I stood there holding the towel in my hand, while the water dripped from my hair to my back and onto the tiles. I looked at Kaka. His face was now hidden behind the pages of his favorite newspaper, the *Sandesh*. I hung my towel on the line and didn't bother to stand in the sun to dry my hair.

I searched the house for Raju, looking in all the rooms and even in the closet where we kept extra mattresses and pillows. I checked under the beds and in the living room corner behind the big couch. I searched the garden, thinking he might be hiding behind the water tank. He wasn't there. I looked up the *badam* tree and the mango tree, but he was not sitting on a branch. Raju had disappeared.

"Mommy, have you seen Raju?" I asked.

"No. Mela has been fussy. Take her in the garden for a few minutes so Pappa and I can finish packing the last two suitcases."

I grabbed Mela and went to the kitchen. Kaki was roasting dry cream of wheat cereal. Before I could ask her if she'd seen Raju, Mela clapped her hands, and squealed, "*Shiro, shiro*, Kaki is making *shiro* for me!"

"For you and Seema and Raju and Uma," Kaki said.

Just as I was asking, "Have you seen Raju?" Kaki added sweetened saffron milk to the cream of wheat and it sizzled, singing *chummm*, puffing steam, and drowning my question. She began stirring it and asked, "What did you say, Seema?"

I knew Kaki had to concentrate on making *shiro* or else it would burn, so I answered, "Nothing," and took Mela out into the garden. I checked the garden one more time, but Raju wasn't there.

That morning slipped from my hand like a butterfly. It had flown away before I could catch it. I wandered through the house and garden searching for Raju. I wanted to talk to Raju alone, but never got a chance. By the time he got home in the afternoon, the house filled with neighbors and friends who'd come to say good-bye. Many of them brought coconuts for good luck, and before we left there were at least two dozen coconuts piled up on one side of our front lobby. Some of them had swastikas drawn on them and some had the sacred sound *om* written on them with red vermilion powder. I remembered three years ago when one of our neighbor's sons had gotten married and they'd drawn two gigantic swastikas on each side of their entrance. I had asked Dadaji, "Why have they drawn swastikas?"

"To bless the couple. The swastika symbolizes good things."

At the time I hadn't thought much of our conversation, but now, seeing the swastikas on the coconuts reminded me of how fortunate we were to have so many people sending us off with such heartfelt good wishes.

I only wished that they'd brought the coconuts a few days earlier so Dadima could have made cardamom-flavored coconut-and-milk candy for us.

Uma gave me a painting in an ivory-colored frame.

"I painted it," she said.

"'Our Home in the Morning.'" I whispered the title as I looked at it. Our garden with the bed of *parijat* flowers and the mango tree with our house in the background looked so real that I thought Raju might walk through the garden gate any minute.

"Do you like it?"

"Uma, it is so beautiful, so real."

"I wanted to capture a sunrise for you, just the way we see it from our house," she said, pointing at the eastern sky bright as bougainvillea blossoms with the sun peeking its forehead over the horizon. I wanted to thank her, but no words came out. I didn't realize that I was trembling until she hugged me.

Uma and I wrapped the painting in a newspaper and I put it in my handbag. I wanted to keep it safe with me.

An hour before we left for the airport, Raju returned. I tied a *rakhi* on his wrist, even though Rakshabandhan was more than a month away.

"I'll be the only one with a *rakhi*," he said.

"You can take it off and have Uma tie it again on Rakshabandhan," I said.

"No. I'll just keep it," he said, playing with the *rakhi's* string, his head bowed. I thought I saw tears hiding under his long lashes.

On the way to the airport, Raju rode in a taxi with me. "Seema, when you come back you'll be talking first-class English," he said.

"And you?" I asked.

"Third-class, as usual."

"You're so good at English. I could never do better than you."

"You will. Wait a month or two. With your American accent I won't even know what you're talking about when you call."

"Why would I talk to you in English? I'll always talk to you in Gujarati."

"You'll forget Gujarati as quickly as you'll forget us," he said.

I didn't answer. He looked at me and grinned. "Just teasing," he said.

"Don't."

At the airport when I bowed down to Kaki, she put her arms around me and said, "Seema, no matter which corner of the world you may go and live in, our hearts will always be open for you."

I buried my face in the folds of her sari.

I said good-bye to Raju last. Neither one of us spoke. We captured each other's gaze for a moment before I turned around and walked away with Pappa, Mommy, and Mela.

Three

We changed planes in Mumbai. When we got on the jumbo jet that was flying us to Amsterdam, I was surprised by its size. Each row was ten seats across, and I couldn't see where the rows ended. "Mommy, this is as big as a ship, isn't it?" I asked softly.

"It is," Mommy said.

"Seema, are we going to sail on a ship through the sky?" Mela asked. A few passengers around us laughed.

I didn't answer.

"Is this a ship that sails through the sky?" Mela asked again.

"It is," I whispered.

It was after midnight when the plane took off. Mommy, Pappa, and Mela fell asleep, but I kept wiggling in my seat. The main cabin lights were turned off and no one talked.

In the plane my mind tossed back and forth like a Ping-Pong ball between India and America. Not long ago, Iowa City had seemed like a place in a story. Soon, I was going to be in that story, and I wondered how long it would take before my home town, Vishanagar, would begin to feel like a fairy tale.

America was everything I'd heard it would be, and yet nothing could have prepared me for America. What struck me the most was that everything was big. Not only were the roads four lanes wide, but the gas stations had eight pumps. The city was dressed like an elegant lady, and the tops of the buildings seemed to have conversations with clouds. Stores were so large that they were never crowded. I remembered Vishanagar's bazaar, where people brushed against my shoulder as they walked past me. Here, there was space and no people to fill it. Where were they all?

We rented a house from a professor who was on a year-long sabbatical. In the new house I had my own room wall-papered in a pink-and-blue pastel design with ducks, geese, and sprays of blue flowers. The matching checkerboard curtains were crisp and the comforter on the bed was fluffy and soft. It was perfect, but I didn't have anyone to share it with. I replaced the comforter on the bed with

Nanima's blue silk blanket. I unwrapped the picture Uma had given me and put it on top of the chest of drawers. As I lingered in front of the painting, I began to feel like I was sharing my room with Uma like I used to in India.

The long window of my room faced the backyard where a circle of yellow marigolds surrounded a clump of red zinnias. The lawn was green and so were the trees. I wondered what the large tree with the white bark was called. Its leaves shimmered and made the same rippling sound as the *pipul* tree did in our school yard, but it wasn't a *pipul*. The *pipul* had heart-shaped leaves with pointy ends, and this tree had oblong leaves with rounded edges.

At night as I lay in bed, I didn't like my room as much as I'd liked it during the day. I was lonely. Even though it wasn't cold, I snuggled up to the extra pillow and pulled my blanket all the way up to my chin. I don't know when I fell asleep, but the next thing I heard was Mommy saying, "Seema, Seema, wake up."

I woke up shivering. Mommy held me in her arms, and I told her about my dream.

"Mommy, I was flying and the sky was dark and below me was the dark ocean. The thundering waves of the ocean were trying to catch me. They almost did catch me. There were sharks. Big ones with jaws of shining steel."

"You were screaming."

"Was I?"

"Yes. That's why I came in. You were shaking like a dry *pipul* leaf. Go back to sleep."

I held on to her.

"Do you want me to sing a *shloka*?" she asked.

"Yes."

She sat on my bed and sang the same *shloka* that Dadima used to sing.

My heart was full of fear, and yet it had never felt emptier. So, I just listened to Mommy's singing and held tightly to her arm.

The next day as I unpacked my suitcases, I spotted the handkerchief that Mukta had given me. I sat there thinking about Mukta, her mother, her house, and her family. My room was bright and cheerful, and yet I could picture her dark and gloomy home vividly. Dadaji used to say that the real eyes are the mind's eyes. I knew I was seeing with my mind's eyes.

I took the handkerchief and laid it gently in the drawer and put my clothes on top of it. Maybe burying the handkerchief would help me forget about Mukta, but I was wrong. It was impossible to bury her memory.

Every morning when I got up I looked out the window, hoping to find an oblong bed of white *parijat* flowers with orange stems. I didn't see them, but there were so many other trees and plants that were nameless to me. Who can tell me about the plants and flowers that grow in this garden? I wondered. Sometimes I saw a neighbor lady working in her garden. It was hard to see her face, for she was always bent over, but maybe someday I could meet her. Someday when I could speak better English I could ask her about the flowers.

The first two weeks passed in a blur. Everything we did was new and different. Instead of washing clothes by hand, we washed and dried them in a machine; instead of sweeping floors with a broom, we cleaned them with a vacuum cleaner; instead of listening to news in Gujarati, we listened to the news in English; and instead of seeing so many people on the street, we only saw a few when we went for a walk.

Of all the new things that we did, shopping for groceries was the most interesting. In the supermarket there were frozen dinners, soup in a can, seven different types of milk, more than ten flavors of yogurt, and twenty flavors of ice cream. There was cereal with nuts and cereal with fruit and there was cereal with lots of sugar. There were packages and bottles and containers and cartons all over the store lined up neatly as if they were ready for inspection. It was good to have so many choices, but it was hard to decide what to get.

When we were out shopping, Mommy would try to speak to me in English the whole time, so that I would become more comfortable with the language by the time school started. Mommy had studied English at university, and she sounded first-class to me. She laughed when I told her. "Well, maybe second-class, now, but we will both be speaking English fluently in a few months, wait and see."

In the supermarket checkout line no one brought cotton bags from home because they all got as many sturdy brown bags or plastic bags as they wanted. "Dadima would love this store," I said to Mommy one day. The day was hot, but the bus we were riding in was air-conditioned.

"She would. So many things to choose from!"

"More than that, think how happy she would be to get all these crisp paper bags. She always uses flimsy paper bags over and over again until they fall apart."

"She might buy more groceries just so she could get more bags," Mommy said.

"I think she might."

We reached our stop, and while we walked to our house I said to Mommy, "Do you think someday we'll get a car too? Then we won't have to carry all the heavy stuff on the bus."

"We don't need a car. In India we bought fresh fruits and vegetables every day and we didn't need a car. Here we shop once a week so we don't need a car at all."

Mommy was right. We didn't need a car, but I wanted one like everyone else.

* * *

After our first four weeks in Iowa City, all the new things that I had found so fascinating in the beginning were not fascinating anymore. The machines did the work, but they couldn't talk to us. The only person I could talk to all day was Mommy. Pappa was busy with his work, and at night Mela wanted to play with him; by the time Mela went to sleep, Pappa was tired and went to bed.

I noticed that the days that had stretched out like a sari when we first arrived were getting shorter, as if someone were clipping a little off bit by bit. I wondered how short the days would become before they became long again. School had already started in India. Here school was start-ing in two weeks, but it was hard to wait that long with nothing to do. Sometimes in the middle of the afternoon I lay on the couch, staring at the ceiling and walls. They were smooth and clean, as if someone had just finished painting them, and there was never anything interesting to spot.

In India there were cracks on the ceilings and paint peel-ing on the walls, making rivers, puddles, and whatever else you could imagine. Raju and I used to play a game called Find What I See. If I saw a patch of wall where paint had peeled off in the shape of a bird, I'd say, "I see a bird," and then he had to find it. Sometimes a row of ants marched along the wall and sometimes a stubborn lizard hung on the ceiling. I didn't like lizards, with their glassy eyes.

The tiles in our house in India were beige with lots of

brown flecks and a few gold ones, which sparkled in the sunlight. On hot summer afternoons Raju and I loved to search for all the gold flecks, pretending they were made out of real gold. The more each of us found, the richer we were. Here the floors were covered in a plain tan carpet, and there were no gold flecks to count.

"Mommy, are you happy here? Do you wish we were in India?" I asked her one evening while she was kneading dough. She paused.

"Why do you ask?"

I shrugged my shoulders.

"It's different, but I like it. Do you like it?" she said.

"I don't know."

"It's a big change for you, but give it a chance. Once school starts and you make friends, it will be better," she said, returning to her work.

I looked outside and saw that the sun was still bright. "Is it okay if Mela and I walk to the park? We'll be back in an hour," I said.

The park was only three streets down, and around the corner. When we'd walked one block a ball suddenly rolled toward us. Mela picked it up and threw it to the girl who had missed the basket.

"Thank you," she said.

"No mention," I said. When she replied with a puzzled expression, I remembered Pappa had once told me that in

America people say *You are welcome* instead of *No mention.* "You are welcome," I said.

She smiled and nodded and her blue eyes brightened as her confusion cleared away.

"Can we play with her?" Mela asked in Gujarati.

Before I could answer, the girl threw the ball toward Mela, and Mela picked it up.

"I'm Jennifer. What's your name?" she asked.

"My name is Mela Trivedi." Mela knew three sentences in English. Her name, her age, and our address. Mommy had taught her those so if she ever got lost, she could ask for help.

Jennifer looked at me. "My name . . . I'm Seema," I said. "You live here this house?"

"No. This is my uncle's house. My house is six blocks away on the other side."

Mela was holding Jennifer's ball, and I told her in Gujarati that she should give it back to Jennifer.

"She gave it to me. Why can't I throw it in the basket?" Mela asked.

"What is she asking? Does she want to play?" Jennifer asked.

I hid my embarrassment by keeping my gaze down on Mela's face.

Mela caught the word *play* and nodded her head. "Play. My play."

"You can shoot the ball in the basket," Jennifer said, motioning with her hand.

When Mela held the ball above her head to shoot it, it dropped behind her and rolled away. A tall girl who was crossing the street picked it up. She began bouncing the ball, and her touch seem to turn it into her dance partner.

"Ria, throw it to Mali," Jennifer said to the girl.

"I am not Mali," Mela said to me, stomping her foot. She wouldn't catch the ball either.

"Her name Mela. *Mali* 'gardener' in my language," I said.

"I'm sorry, Mela. You have a very pretty name," Jennifer said, kneeling down so she was eye to eye with Mela and handing her the ball.

Mela gave her a smile as big as the basketball.

Then she tried to throw the ball, but it didn't even touch the bottom of the basket. Ria picked her up and gave her a piggyback to the net. Mela threw the ball and made a basket. Jennifer began clapping, and so I did too. Mela looked very pleased with herself.

"Where do you live?" Ria asked.

"Next street," I said, pointing toward our house.

"Ria, this is Seema," Jennifer said.

"My name is Mela and I am four," Mela said.

"Hi, Seema. Hi, four-year-old Mela. Do you want to play with us?" Ria said.

"I play not basketball," I said.

"It's easy."

"I play basketball," Mela said.

While playing, I noticed that Ria's short hair was tightly curled. If those curls were opened up like a fan, they would reach her shoulders. Her skin was not as white as Jennifer's but the color of saffron-and-nutmeg rice pudding, and her large eyes were twinkling with naughtiness. Jennifer's hair was the color of sweet papaya and hung straight down her back, and her eyes were clear water-mirrors that reflected the sky.

Ria asked me, "Do you know Priya Ray or Asha Mehta?"

"No," I said.

"They go to our school and their parents are from India," Jennifer said. "Do you know any other kids?"

"I not know anyone," I said.

"You know us," Ria said, pointing at Jennifer and herself.

"Yes," I said, and smiled.

Question after question bubbled in my mind. I wished I could speak English fluently. I strung one more sentence together. "How big the classes?"

"About twenty-four, twenty-five," Ria said.

"In India, we fifty in one class."

"That's big."

"You get how much homework?"

"A lot," Jennifer said.

"I work hard. I fear school very difficult here. My English not good," I said.

Ria and Jennifer looked at each other. "Your English is fine," Jennifer said.

"I hope the three of us are in the same class," Ria said.

"Yes, same class, very nice," I said.

An hour went by so fast that Mela and I didn't have time to go to the park. When we got home I had so much to tell Pappa and Mommy that I couldn't finish a bowl of rice and dal. "Ria said our principal dresses up in strange costumes like a cow or a pig for one of the holidays."

"Good thing he doesn't do that every day," Pappa said.

"No, for Hallo-een or Hollo-ween or something like that. It comes on the thirty-first of October. Everyone dresses up that day."

"I want to be a princess," Mela said.

"Fine," I said. "Ria is going to be a pumpkin. Jennifer doesn't know what she wants to be."

"How can Ria be a pumpkin?" Mommy said.

"Why not?" I said.

"Because a pumpkin is round and short and you told us that she's very tall," Mommy said.

"Then it's a challenge," Pappa said.

"I want to be a princess," Mela said.

"I told you, you can be a princess," I said. "What can I be?"

"Not a princess. I'm going to be a princess," Mela said.

"*O bhaisab!* Will you let me talk? If I can't dress up, then who will take you out and how will you get peppermints and chocolate?" I said.

"I want peppermint. Jennifar will give me peppermint."

"It's not Jenni*far*, it's Jenni*fer*," I said.

Mela didn't answer me. Instead, she said, "Pappa, I want chocolate, now."

"Let's finish eating," Mommy said. And then in Hindi she said to me, "We'll talk about this holiday after the little one goes to bed." Mela didn't understand Hindi, but she had not forgotten about the candy, and after dinner Pappa gave us each a piece of chocolate.

That night I asked, "Mommy, can you make me a costume?"

"I don't know how to sew," Mommy said.

"Can't you sew me anything?"

"Have you ever seen me make a single stitch?"

"No. I wish Kaki were here. She would've made me anything I wanted. Why didn't you learn from her?" I asked.

Mommy didn't reply. I felt miserable hurting her feelings and sat there thinking about what I could say to make her feel better. After a while I said, "It's fine if you can't sew. October thirty-first is still far away and I'm sure we can think of something."

Mommy smiled and squeezed my hand.

Before school started I got to see Ria and Jennifer a few more times. Slowly, talking in English was getting easier. The night before the first day of school I said to Pappa, "I hope Ria, Jennifer, and I are in the same class."

"How many sixth-grade classes are there?" he asked.

"Four or five, I'm not sure. Why?"

"Well, the probability of all three of you being in the same class is . . ."

Before he could say anymore I interrupted. "Don't tell me about the probability. I'm hoping that we are all in same class, that's all."

"Sometimes all that calculation is of no use," Mommy said.

"Calculations are always of use," he said.

"Only in your laboratory, Pappa."

"And what if someday you want to work in a laboratory?"

"I'm not going to look at bugs through a microscope, the way you do."

"They're called bacteria, and they're fun," he said.

"I don't want a share of your fun. You can have it all," I said.

"I will."

For those few minutes while we talked I didn't worry about school, but that night, in bed, all the fear that I'd pressed so hard in my heart began to balloon.

four

I was glad my school, Grant Elementary, started at eight in the morning, leaving no time for my fear to swell again. All my life Raju and I had left for school at ten-thirty, except on Saturday mornings. Saturdays, we had four hours of morning school. In Iowa City there was no school on Saturdays.

I gulped down the milk and whole-wheat bread that Mommy had set on the table. "Pappa, let's go," I said, wiping my face.

When we reached the school, the hundreds of children in bright clothes made me feel like I had come to a giant party. I tried to imagine all of them in school uniforms like the ones Raju and I wore in Vishanagar.

My hand clung to Pappa's arm while my eyes searched for Jennifer and Ria. I didn't see either one of them. Pappa said, "Let me walk you to your class."

The classroom was buzzing with activity. All the students' shiny backpacks matched their excited faces. Everyone had someone to greet, someone to talk to, someone to laugh with, someone to hug, except me. I tightened my grip on Pappa, wishing he were Raju; then we could sit together and it wouldn't be so bad.

"Are you ready?" Pappa asked.

I thought of what Mommy had told me the night before: *Be thoughtful and kind, Seema, and friends will follow as clouds follow wind.*

"I'm ready, Pappa," I said, and walked into the class. Not only was my throat dry, but my mouth and even my lips were dry. I sat at the first empty desk I saw. Before I could look around, a lady walked toward me. Had I done something wrong? I wondered. She was young, with hair so golden that it reminded me of the flame of the *diya*, a prayer lamp that Dadima lighted every day. "You must be Seema Trivedi," she said.

"Yes," I whispered so quietly that I couldn't hear my own voice.

"I'm Ms. Wilson, your teacher. I'm glad to have you in my class."

Before I could arrange a reply in English, someone

called her. After talking to Jennifer and Ria I was getting better at stringing words together in English. Still, I always thought in Gujarati first and then translated into English. I wanted to say, *I'm also glad to be here*, but I couldn't think fast enough.

Ms. Wilson introduced herself to the class and then she announced, "This is the first day of class and for everyone this is a new beginning. However, there are two students who are new to our school. Sam Bally, who moved here from California, and Seema Trivedi, who came all the way from India." When I heard Ms. Wilson say my name I stood up. Everyone stared at me.

She continued, "Let us all welcome them to Grant Elementary school. I'm glad they're in our class and I hope you'll help them out and make their transition easy."

I was still standing up. As I waited for Ms. Wilson to ask me to sit down, I looked around and realized that Sam Bally had not stood up. I didn't know what to do.

"Seema, do you want to say something?" Ms. Wilson asked.

"No . . . Yes . . . I . . . I . . . sit down?"

"Yes, you may sit down," she said. I was so embarrassed that I wanted to hide my face in my hands and become invisible. As I sat down I heard a snicker from behind me, and my face turned warm with shame and anger. Instead of sitting down, I wished I could run away from the class, from the school, from the country, back to my old school. I wouldn't complain even if they put me next to Mukta.

In India when the teacher said my name I stood to show my respect. During Ms. Wilson's class the students didn't get up when they asked a question or when she called on them. They answered sitting down! Since there were only twenty-two students in the class, everyone got a chance to talk to Ms. Wilson. They seemed to like her and she seemed to like all of them, but they didn't get up to show their respect.

Ms. Wilson gave us a lot of instructions on our first day of school. I wished Jennifer and Ria were in my class, because I understood so little. In history we were going to start by studying World War II. Sam Bally was very excited and kept asking questions. Although we were both new students, we were not alike. The class felt like a fast-moving train; Sam Bally had hopped onto it, while I was still standing on a platform frantically searching for my ticket.

By the time recess came my frustration turned to anger. I'm so dumb that I will never learn English. If I never learn English how am I going to pass the sixth grade? I wished I had stayed back in India as Dadaji and Kaka had wanted me to.

When I walked toward the cafeteria for lunch break,

I noticed a nauseating smell. It got stronger as I got closer to it. I realized it was the smell of food I'd never had in my life. I tried not to inhale the smell, but the more I thought about not inhaling it, the more I was overcome by it. The cafeteria was huge and everyone had a place to sit down. As soon as I walked in I heard, "Seema, Seema, come here!" It was Jennifer, waving. "Come, eat with us."

Jennifer was sitting with Ria and three other girls. I hesitated for a second, but she and Ria made room for me to sit right between the two of them. I looked at their lunches. They were small. They each had a sandwich, fruit, a cookie, and juice. Once I opened my lunch the strange odor was replaced by the whiff of cumin, ginger, and red pepper. I wondered if anyone thought my food smelled strange. Mommy had packed me *rotli* bread, spicy peas, rice, plain yogurt, mango pickles that we had brought from India, and sweet *shiro*, made of semolina roasted in butter and flavored with cardamom and saffron. In India our biggest meal was lunch. Pappa had told Mommy to pack a small lunch for me, and yet it was too big. I couldn't finish half of my food. At lunch everyone talked so fast that I understood very little.

I had math and science that afternoon, and it was a relief. Unlike words, the equations were written and solved the same way in America as they were written and solved in India. Scientific principles were universal, and the pull of gravity was the same in America as it was in India. I grasped more and learned more than I had in the morning.

When I walked out of Grant Elementary, Mommy and Mela were waiting for me. "How was the first day?" Mommy asked.

"Not very good, not very bad," I said.

"Tell me," Mommy said.

I told Mommy how nice Ms. Wilson was, how little I understood the instructions, how I ate lunch with Jennifer and Ria, and how easy math was. But I didn't tell Mommy how miserable I felt in the morning, because she'd worry about me and yet she could do nothing about it. "I missed Raju," I told Mommy and Pappa that evening. They nodded as if they understood, but I wondered if they really understood how much I wanted him to be with me.

The next morning I asked Mommy if I could take a sandwich for lunch. She made me a cheese-and-tomato sandwich, and at lunch I ate what everyone else was eating. It felt comfortable to eat a sandwich, even though I preferred *rotli* with spicy vegetables.

In school, Ms. Wilson made sure I understood my assignments. After she gave instructions to the class and they began their work, she sat next to me and explained what she wanted me to do. Her voice was sweet and kind, like that of Mukta's mommy. They were two different people living in different countries and yet they were so much alike.

On the third day of class Ms. Wilson gave us some math problems. We were reviewing last year's math, and it was easy. "Does anyone have the answer for problem number five?" she asked.

I looked around. No one had their hand up. I gingerly raised my hand.

"Yes, Seema. What did you get?"

"One *lakh*," I said.

"One what?" Ms. Wilson asked.

"One *lakh*," I repeated.

"I am afraid I don't understand you," she said.

"Maybe I did it wrong," I said, confused.

"Can you show the class how you did it?"

I got up. My hand was shaking as I wrote on the blackboard. Between me and the blackboard was my warm breath, which made me break out in a sweat. I wrote down the problem the way I had done it. I underlined my answer: 1,00000.

"You're right," Ms. Wilson said, "but in your answer you need to put the comma after the second zero."

"I put comma after one because it is one *lakh*," I said.

"I'm sorry. I don't know what you're saying. In English it's called one hundred thousand."

I stood there like a wooden doll, unable to move or breathe.

"You can sit down," Ms. Wilson said. I don't know how I got back to my desk.

When I went home, I wrote *100000* without adding a comma and asked Mommy what it was called. She looked at me and said, "*Kem*, why Seema, don't you know that is one *lakh*?"

"What is a *lakh* in English?" I asked.

Mommy's brow became tense and after a few seconds she said, "A *lakh* is a *lakh*, isn't it?"

"It isn't. Ms. Wilson said that this is called 'one hundred thousand,'" I said, adding a comma after the second zero.

"She must be right."

"If I don't even know the numbers, how am I going to learn math?"

"You will learn soon. We will all learn soon," she said.

That night I talked to Pappa about what had happened in school. He had heard about a hundred thousand and a million when he was here the last time, but had forgotten about it.

"But Pappa, in India even the *Times of India* uses *lakh*s and *crore*s. If they are not English words why do they use them?"

"Everyone in India knows *lakh*s and *crore*s. It is always hard to count in another language," he said.

"What do you mean? If you can read and write in English, why can't you count in it?"

"I don't know why, but I can never count in English. All day long I think and talk with people in English. I write my papers in English and I present them in English, but I still count in Gujarati, and I still use the three sections of each finger to count by hand."

"Then how do people understand what numbers you're talking about?"

"I convert it into English before I say it."

If Pappa had a problem counting in English, I knew I would. I wondered if I would forever be counting in Gujarati and converting it into English.

That night I wrote a letter before I went to bed.

Dear Raju,

I wish you were here. Without you, life here is like playing in a monsoon rain without a friend. Even those things that were easy for me in India are tough here. Did you know that there aren't lakhs *and* crores *in English? They are Indian words used in India and no one understands them here. I can do math really fast in my head, faster than anyone here, because Dadaji made us do our times table every night. Students in my class are surprised that I can calculate seventeen times eight in my head. Also, because they don't count on each section of each finger, they can only count up to ten on their fingers instead of thirty.*

Numbers are not the only confusing thing. Just when you think you know the right English word it turns out to be wrong. Mommy wanted to buy brinjal, *but it's called eggplant here. Lady fingers are called okras. Potato wafers are called potato chips, and biscuits are called cookies. Tomato sauce is ketchup, and peppermint is candy. Not only that, but lady fingers, wafers, biscuits, tomato sauce, and peppermint are something else altogether! When I try to smooth it all out in my mind, I get all knotted up.*

There are drinks here I'd never heard of, like apple cider and Kool-Aid. Some of the colors of Kool-Aid, brilliant blue and dark green, remind me of a tie-dye bandhani *sari. Can you imagine drinking such stuff? The drinks we're used to, like rose water sherbet and mango sherbet, are found nowhere in America. Here sherbets are not drinks, but a cross between ice cream and snow cones.*

I'm sorry if I've confused you. Someday I will get it all right and then I will explain it to you all over again.

How's school? What are you learning about? How is your running going? Write to me soon.

Love,

Seema

Five weeks of school had passed, and I noticed that every day when I came home, the sun was getting lower and lower in the sky, and it was getting cooler. One day I saw some leaves that had turned red. I picked up two and brought them home to show Mommy. She thought they were pretty, and we put them in a glass jar. A few days later more trees were changing colors. It was as if the trees were tired of wearing their green saris and were trying on red, brown, yellow, and purple ones.

The mornings were getting colder, and Mommy made me bundle up, but during the day it warmed up and the sun shone brightly. In math we had pretests before each chapter, and I was getting a hundred percent on them. One day Ms. Wilson asked me, "Seema, your math skills are excellent! How about switching to advanced math?"

"Can I do that?" I wondered aloud.

"Of course you can. I'll talk to Mrs. Kramer about your joining her class."

At lunch recess, as soon as I saw Jennifer, I blurted, "Ms. Wilson asked me to take advanced math."

"Seema, that's great. Are you going to do it?"

"I said yes to Ms. Wilson, so I guess I have to. I still struggle with English, but not as much as I used to."

"You're doing first-class in English too," she said. We both laughed.

* * *

I realized that even though I missed everyone in India, especially Raju, I wasn't miserable in Iowa City. One day when I came home from school, Mommy gave me a letter. I knew right away it was from Mukta. The letter had carried her scent across the ocean. I sat down by the window in the light of golden leaves.

Dear Seema,

I asked Raju if you and your family had reached America. He told me that you had and you are all doing well. I think of you every day and imagine what kind of school you must be going to.

I had stopped going to school because my kaki is sick with tuberculosis and it costs a lot of money to treat her. But our principal, Tarlaben, told me that a family had paid my entire year's fees and book money so I can return to school. When I asked her who it was, she said that the donor wanted to remain anonymous. Even though I don't know who the donor was, I pray for the family. The school uniforms that you gave me have made all the difference. I don't have to wear the same uniform all week and wash it on Saturday after-noon. I've been using two of them and keeping one for special occasions like the Independence Day parade on the fifteenth of August.

Do you know when you'll be back? I wait for your return and all the stories you can tell me. Write me a long letter with all the things you have seen and felt. That way I can be there too.

Your loving friend,

Mukta

I read Mukta's letter twice, folded it up, and slipped it into the bottom of my drawer where I had put her hand-kerchief. I was happy that she was going to school, but I didn't like to read about her *kaki* having tuberculosis. Pappa's only sister had died from it when she was twenty years old. Dadima had told me that in the old times it was called a *rajrog*, a king's disease, because it cost so much to cure. I wondered how Mukta's family could afford it. Mommy asked me how Mukta was and I said she was fine. I didn't feel like telling her about Mukta's *kaki* being sick. I thought that the less I talked about Mukta and her fam-ily, the faster I could forget about them.

The days hurried by as if they were late for a party and

the nights hung around like they had nowhere else to go. On some days the sun was brilliant and those days sparkled; on other days I could look at the sun without squinting my eyes. What use is the sun when it is as mellow as the moon? I thought. At least the moon was lovely, but the afternoon sun draped in gray clouds could never be lovely.

Pappa was very busy at work, and when he got home, it was always dark. One day when I came home from school, Mommy said, "Seema, let's go get some groceries while it's still light."

"Can I stay at home?" I asked.

"I can't do it alone. I need you."

"You can leave Mela with me."

"I want to go with Mommy," Mela said.

"Let's all go," Mommy said.

Mommy quickly loaded milk, juice, bananas, apples, an eggplant, a cauliflower, a few cans of chickpeas, and bread into the cart. By the time we'd paid and walked out, the sun had set and the wind was furious. I was reminded of the sandstorms we used to get before the monsoon in India. As we waited for the bus the wind howled, and each blast was icier than the last. Even through gloves my hands were freezing, and the grocery bag was getting heavier. I glanced at the store, where shoppers were out in the cold for a few seconds before entering the store or heading back to their cars. Mommy knew what I was thinking and said, "Days like this are not going to come often, Seema. We don't need a car."

"It will get colder than this, Mommy. Everyone at school says so, and there will be snow."

"Colder than this? I don't think so."

"A lot colder than this. It's only October, and the coldest month is January. That's what Jennifer told me."

Mommy didn't reply.

"I'm cold," Mela said.

"Would you like a candy?" I asked.

"*Na*, I'm cold. I want to go home," she said, and started crying.

"Do you want to play a guessing game?" I asked.

"*NA.*"

"How about a story? The one that Dadima used to tell us?"

"*NA, NA, NA.* I want to go home. NOW," Mela said, and pulled Mommy's hand. Mommy almost lost her balance.

"Mela, *choop ker*, be quiet. If you open your mouth once more, I'll slap you," Mommy said.

Mela was so shocked that she stopped crying and said, "Slap me like Kaka slapped Raju?" I didn't know Mela had seen Kaka slap Raju and remembered it after all these months.

We rode quietly in the bus, but as soon as we got home Mommy started crying, and so did Mela. I got them both some water to drink, and after a while Mommy took Mela in her lap.

"Are you okay, Mommy?" I asked.

"I'm miserable," she said. "I don't know why we're in this dark, depressing cave. I feel so trapped. If I go out, the cold grabs me, and if I stay in, I suffocate. My feet are freezing, my hands never warm up, and my back is stiff. I sleep with two pairs of socks. I, who never owned a pair of socks for thirty-five years! I never liked cold, and now I hate it, I hate it."

"It will be all right, Mommy. It will be," I said.

"How can it be? You said it is going to get colder. What are Mela and I going to do cooped up in the house all day? I miss India. I miss the markets, the crowds, the music, our language, our books, the sunshine and its warmth. I miss our family and our friends. These deserted streets, the darkness of the daytime, the stillness, they choke me."

"I'm sorry, Mommy, I didn't know you were so sad," I said.

Before Mommy could say anything, Mela gave her a kiss. "You're not sad now, Mommy. Are you?"

"No," Mommy said and put her arms around both of us. We all sat quietly for a while on the couch and Mela fell asleep. Mommy and I went in the kitchen. While making tea, Mommy said, "I'm sorry, Seema, for getting so upset. I surprised myself. This must've been boiling inside me for a long time, and the cold and the wind made it spill out. You and your Pappa have something to do here and you both meet new people, learn new things, and do your work, but Mela has no one to play with and I have no one to talk to. In India I didn't know where time went, and here I am, with time laughing in my face."

"You and Mela used to go for walks a lot and meet neighbors. What about that?"

"It's getting colder, and I haven't seen too many people out."

"Can Mela go to a preschool? I can find out which school Ria's brother goes to. He's four, like Mela."

Mommy sat down with a cup of tea. I snuggled up to her. "Do you think Mela knows enough English to be in school?" she asked.

"She does. And once she goes to school she'll learn fast."

Mommy didn't make dinner that night. We called for pizza instead. Someone delivered it in a huge cardboard box. It was hot and delicious. Pappa listened quietly when we told him about our day.

"I'm sorry, Aruna. I have a list of telephone numbers of Indian families in town that I should have given to you," he said.

"Where is the list?" Mommy asked.

"In the office."

"When did you get it?" I asked.

"About a month ago," he replied.

"A month ago?" Mommy and I both shouted together.

"I'm sorry," he said. "I got so busy that I forgot all about it. As soon as I get to work I'll call some of the families."

"Get me the list, that's all. I'll call them. I'm also going to send Mela to preschool," Mommy said.

Pappa nodded and smiled. "Seema, Mommy is as feisty as the day I met her."

"It's the icy wind that has made her feisty," I said. Mommy had been so different that day that I was worried about her.

five

I met Mrs. Milan one day in October. When I came home from school that afternoon Mommy and Mela were raking leaves in the yard with a lady. I couldn't see her face, but her hair was as pretty as silver embroidery on a sari. I'd seen her from my window working in her garden when we first moved, but then she'd disappeared. For two months her house was empty, except occasionally, when someone came to cut the lawn and work in the garden.

When Mommy introduced me to Mrs. Milan, I noticed that she had kind eyes, like Dadima's, and her face was large, with an upturned mouth.

"These are such beautiful leaves. I mailed a few to my cousin in India," I said to Mrs. Milan.

She stopped raking, and put her chin on the top of the rake handle and said, "Are you pulling my leg?"

I looked at her leg. I wasn't touching her leg, so how could I be pulling it? "I'm not pulling your leg," I said.

"So you really sent them to your cousin. What did she think of them?"

"He liked them a lot. He said that after a peacock's feather they were the most beautiful things."

"I suppose leaves don't change colors in India?"

"No. The leaves turn brownish yellow and not all at the same time. Do you get such bright yellows and reds every year?"

"Yes. That's what fall is around here. Some years we have sharper, brighter colors, depending on the spring and the moisture in the ground. The best fall I've seen is in Vermont. It's as if the mountains are on fire. You'd like it."

In school I had seen a map of the United States, and I knew where Vermont was. It was far away. "Someday, I hope I can go to Vermont in the fall," I said.

"You will," she said, putting her arm around me.

When Mommy went in to make some tea, Mela jumped on the leaf pile that she'd made.

"Mela, come out of there," I said. I stole a glance at Mrs. Milan. I thought she'd be angry, but she wasn't.

Her eyes sparkled even more in the setting sun as she

said, "Why? She can't hurt herself in the leaves. You can jump in, too, if you want."

I hesitated. "Jump in, sweet pea. I used to do that all the time," she said.

"Okay," I said, and jumped on the pile.

While Mommy and Mrs. Milan drank chai—spiced Indian tea—they talked. Mrs. Milan had never had chai before, and she liked it a lot. Mela and I had a piece of apple pie that Mrs. Milan had brought. It was tart and sweet, with a flaky crust. It was my first slice of apple pie ever.

I sat at the dining table to do my homework, but one ear was turned to Mommy and Mrs. Milan's talk. Sipping her chai, Mrs. Milan reminisced about her childhood, her large family, and the hardships of the Depression. Her parents had immigrated from Switzerland and her husband's parents had come from Italy. Mommy talked about our family in India and how much we missed them. Outside, the sun had set and it was getting colder and darker, but inside our hearts we were feeling the warmth and light of a new friendship.

That night I took out an extra notebook that I had not used for school and wrote down, *"To pull a leg"—does it mean to tease someone, to make mashakari of someone? I think it does. Mrs. Milan called me "sweet pea." I like that.*

* * *

The leaves were falling by the sackful each day, and some trees were almost bald. One night it rained and rained, and in the morning the few leaves left clinging to the trees made them look like beggars in ragged clothes. I pushed away the image of *neem* trees with warm sunshine dripping between branches.

"Seema, do you know what's on Tuesday?" Mommy asked, as I was putting my lunch box in my backpack.

"No," I said.

"It's Diwali," she said.

"Diwali?" How could I have forgotten Diwali? In India, it didn't matter if Diwali came in October or in November. There I always knew when it was Diwali without anyone telling me and without looking at any calendar, because Diwali meant bazaars full of bright silk saris and embroidered dress materials. Diwali meant sweet shops filled with red, green, and yellow gift boxes. Diwali meant jewelry shops' showcases full of gold necklaces and bangles.

How had Diwali snuck up so quietly? It had come without Mommy Diwali-cleaning the house as she did in India. It had come without Pappa buying all the fireworks and dividing them among Uma, Raju, and me, and keeping some sparklers for Mela and some big rockets and bombs for himself. It had come without anyone making spicy *fafda* and sweet *ghugra* with plump raisins to eat.

"Seema, it is Diwali next Tuesday," Mommy repeated.

"What are we doing to celebrate?" I asked.

"I'm making *fafda* and *ghugra* and we're going to make a special dinner on Diwali night."

"Yes," I said, and slipped out the door. On the way to school I thought about the last Diwali. Uma and I had hidden our fireworks from Raju, but he'd found them. Every day he stole a couple packages of sparklers, or tiny bombs, or a *chakerdi* that swirled on the floor, streaming sparkles. We caught Raju one day when he thought Uma and I were not home. In the storage room Raju's back was turned toward the door and his rear end was sticking out. As he grabbed the sparkler packets, Uma and I came from behind and grabbed his arms and twisted them. He let out a shriek and dropped the boxes. The year before that, Uma and I had hidden our fireworks in the closet where we stored extra pillows, blankets, and mattresses. When Dadima found out about it, she was so upset that she took our fireworks away. Two days before Diwali she gave them all back to us, as we knew she would. Dadima could never stay angry.

On the Diwali Day at school I kept thinking about how much fun Uma and Raju must be having, and wished I was there. Then I realized that they must be wishing the same thing, and maybe this Diwali would not be much fun for them either. I wondered about Mukta and her family. Did they have any fun at Diwali? And what about Mukta's *kaki*? Was her tuberculosis better or worse?"

I hurried home, with one dark cloud following me overhead.

"Can we light a few *diya* lamps?" I asked as soon as I walked through the door.

"We don't have any *diya*s. How about lighting some candles?" Mommy said.

"No, that's okay," I said, and went up to my room. I stared out the window. The last light of the day was lingering on as if the sun felt guilty about setting. Diwali always fell on a new-moon night, and so I knew the moon wouldn't come up tonight. In India when the night turned dark, we would take out small clay containers and fill them with oil and a long cotton wick. Dipping one end of the wick in the oil and keeping the other end hanging out, we would get one hundred *diya*s ready and place them all around the terrace and balcony ledges. Mommy, Uma, and Pappa would light them, and the lamps would twinkle in the moonless night. Nothing was more beautiful than standing on the terrace admiring the *diya*s twinkling below and the stars twinkling above.

"We have two candles that we can light," I heard Mommy saying as she walked into my room.

I wiped the tears away before I turned around.

"Yes, let's do that," I said, with great effort.

As soon as we put the candles outside the wind blew

them out. We lit them again and the same thing happened. "It won't do," Mommy said.

She came in and collapsed in a chair.

"I have an idea," I said. "Why don't we light candles for our dinner table?"

"It's not the same, but it would be pretty to eat dinner by candlelight," she admitted.

"Dadima always had *diya*s. These are not *diya*s," Mela said, when she saw candles on the table.

"Like *diya*s, candles give us light and that is important, because Diwali is the festival of lights," Mommy reminded her. "We light *diya*s and pray that we have lights in our homes as well as in our hearts."

"When we light the candles can we pray?" Mela asked.

"Yes. We will," Mommy said. I saw a smile on her face and it made me happy.

When Pappa came home we said prayers together and then sat down for dinner. Mommy took out stainless-steel plates and bowls that we had brought from India, and the candlelight reflected from their shiny surfaces onto our faces. The rain began thumping on the window while we ate steaming samosas. I dipped mine in the sweet-and-sour chutney and filled my mouth with crisp crust and spicy filling.

That night we called India. Raju said to me, "I have a Rakshabandhan surprise for you."

"Can't you mail it to me?"

"Don't think so. It'll be waiting for you when you get here."

"I may not be back for two years or more," I said.

"The later you come, the larger it will be."

"Give me a hint," I said.

"I just did," he said.

Two months of school had gone by. On the last Sunday of October all four of us went out to get some milk and yogurt. Mommy picked up three cans of chickpeas and I chose chocolate pudding and a jar of peanut butter. When we got off the bus I asked, "Pappa, are we going to get a car?"

"I'm thinking about getting a car," Pappa said. "I talked to Dr. Davis and he said we must have a car."

"We don't need a car. This works. . . ." Before Mommy could finish her sentence, the bottom of her bag tore, and a can of chickpeas hit her foot before rolling away. She fell. *"O bapre!"*

I ran to the house and opened the door while Pappa carried Mommy into the house. She cried in pain, and even though we applied ice to her foot, it swelled up. Pappa rushed to Mrs. Milan, and she drove Mommy to the emergency room. Pappa went with them while I stayed home with Mela.

The car was barely out of the driveway when Mela asked, "When will Mommy come back?"

"Soon," I said.

I was afraid to be alone with Mela in the house and so I kept busy. I put away the groceries while I talked to her. She was getting hungry, so I made her a cheese-and-tomato sandwich. "I don't want cheese-and-tomato sambich," she said.

"Do you want a peanut-butter-and-jelly sandwich?"

"I like peanut butter," she said.

I made her a peanut-butter-and-jelly sandwich. She took one bite and made a fish face. "I don't like it," she said, pushing her plate away.

"You just said you like peanut butter."

"I don't like jelly with it and I don't like peanut butter on bread. I like peanut butter on celery."

"We don't have any celery," I said. "What do you want?"

"*Rotli* and vegetables."

Many times I had rolled Indian bread, *rotli*, and a couple of times I even had made the dough, but I'd never cooked it on the stove. "Eat a sandwich now and when Mommy and Pappa come back you can have *rotli* and vegetables."

"No," she said and stood there pouting.

"Do you want chocolate pudding?"

"Yes. Pudding! Pudding for dinner." She clapped.

So Mela had chocolate pudding and I tried her peanut-butter-and-jelly sandwich. The peanut butter kept getting stuck in my mouth and throat, and I had to take a sip of milk and swoosh it around to gulp the sandwich down. After two bites I threw it away and ate a tomato-and-cheese sandwich. I was glad that I had tried a peanut-butter sandwich at home and not at school. It was always easier to try new things at home when no one was watching.

"When will Mommy and Pappa come home?" Mela asked as she licked the last spoonful of pudding.

"Soon," I said.

After five minutes she asked the same question, and I gave the same answer. All of a sudden she began to cry. Not a soft cry, but a loud cry, as if someone had slapped her hard. "Mela, please. Don't cry," I said.

"I want Mommy!"

"She'll come."

."Now. I want her now."

The evening was falling slowly. Mommy and Pappa had been gone for three hours. I wondered if Mrs. Milan was back. I called her, but no one answered. Mela and I walked to her house and knocked on the door. There was no answer. We knocked again, still no answer. We walked back to our house. By now everything was dark inside. I turned on all the lights, making the kitchen and the living room bright. Mela and I snuggled up on the couch and I told her a story about the brave rabbit that went into the abandoned house and lived there by himself. It was Raju's favorite story, and he used to beg Dadima to tell it to us over and over again. How I used to protest that I didn't want to hear that story, I thought! And now, if by magic Dadima and Raju could be here, I would listen to that story a hundred and one times.

Mela was quiet. I looked at her. She was asleep.

What if Mommy and Pappa don't come back? I thought. What would Mela and I do? I wished we were in India with everyone; then I wouldn't mind Mommy and Pappa leaving us, because we wouldn't be alone. I wished we were still a whole snow cone and not a broken-off lump that was melting away fast.

The phone rang. It was Pappa. "Seema . . . Seema, is that you? Where were—where did you go? I tried—I called a few minutes ago. Why didn't you— Are you all right? Is Mela all right?" His words were spilling out like the beads from a broken necklace.

"We went to Mrs. Milan's house."

"Mrs. who?"

"Mrs. Milan. The one who took you to the emergency room."

"Mrs. Milan is with us. How's Mela?"

"She's asleep. Where's Mommy?" I asked.

"She's with the doctor. We will be home soon."

"How soon?"

"As soon as she gets done. I have to go now. Lock the house and stay inside. Don't go out again," he said, and hung up.

The night had deepened, and I was getting nervous. I thought of turning the TV on, but I was afraid that if the TV was on it would drown out all other sounds. As fearful as I was, I wanted to hear if someone broke in to the house. I sat by Mela on the couch, chewing the end of the pencil that was on the table by the phone. I had to go to the bathroom, but I didn't want to walk down the hallway alone, and the more I sat there thinking about not going to the bathroom, the more I had to go.

I must have fallen asleep, because it was nine o'clock when Pappa woke me up. First I went to the bathroom and then I went to bed.

The next morning Mommy said we were getting a car.

"A shiny new car?" I asked.

"No. A used car."

"Not an old, rusty car," I protested.

"It will be old, but it won't be rusty," Pappa said.

"Promise?"

"You can help select," she said.

A dreadful thought went through my head. Pappa was used to driving on the left side and here they drove on the right side. What if he made a mistake and drove on the wrong side and had an accident?

"Pappa, we can't get a car," I said.

"Why not?"

"Who's going to drive our car?"

"You are," he said.

"I can't. Not until I'm sixteen."

"Then you're right. We can't get a car."

"Pappa!"

"Why are you worried? You know that Pappa and I both know how to drive," Mommy said.

"Look at your foot. How are you going to drive?"

"Soon, I hope," she said.

"But you both drive on the wrong side. What if you make a mistake?"

"We'll be very careful," Pappa promised.

With Mommy's foot all wrapped up in a big bundle, Pappa and I did most of the cooking and cleaning, and Mela tried folding clothes.

We did get a two-year-old car, which looked very new. Pappa drove as if he had been driving in the United States for a long time. Later he told me that when he came here the first time he had driven a lot. As soon as we got the car we went to the mall and bought heavy jackets and boots for the winter. Now we were ready for cold and wind.

Finally it was Halloween. Jennifer gave me her last year's bear costume, which fit snugly. It was drizzling while Mela, Jennifer, and I went around the neighborhood shouting, "Trick or treat!" At first I was scared, especially at one house. When we rang the bell, the door opened slowly with a screechy sound, and a hand with long, sharp nails dangled out from behind it. I grabbed Mela's hand, jumped back, and screamed. Jennifer laughed and said, "Mr. Tobias, you can't scare us." Then a face with fangs peeked around the door. He held out three big candy bars. I looked over my shoulder as I went down the steps of his house. His laughter echoed in the sky.

I came home with more candy than I had ever seen in my life, and it was all mine. I divided it in two piles: in the first pile were the candies I'd tasted before, and in the second were candies I'd never eaten. The second pile was five times as big as the first one. That night as I took out my nightdress, Mukta's handkerchief and letter fell out. I wished I could mail her some candies. Maybe I'll write her a letter, I thought. *Soon, do it soon*, my heart urged.

six

In school Ms. Wilson taught the class the history of Thanksgiving. During dinner I asked Mommy and Pappa, "Did you know that the first Thanksgiving dinner was served at Plymouth in 1621?"

"No, we didn't," Mommy said.

"I did," Mela said. I ignored her.

"The Pilgrims were thankful for a good harvest and celebrated the day with a big feast."

"A big feast," Mela said, with her arms wide apart.

"Why do you keep interrupting?" I said.

"Seema, she's as excited as you are. Let her say a few things," Mommy said.

"Say something. Now!" I told Mela. She was quiet.

"See, she has nothing to say except when I talk, then she starts jabbering."

"How did our Thanksgiving holiday turn into a Complaingiving holiday?" Pappa asked jokingly in English. I noticed that more and more often, we were sprinkling our conversations in Gujarati with English words and phrases.

"I don't know. Pappa, Jennifer is going to her grandparents' house in Wisconsin, and Ria is going to her aunt and uncle's house in Chicago. Where can we go?"

"India," Mela said.

"It's too far," I said.

"Dr. and Mrs. Davis have invited us for Thanksgiving dinner," Mommy said.

"Really?"

"We're going for a feast! We're going for a feast!" Mela sang and clapped.

On Thanksgiving day I wore a mango-colored silk dress. Mommy French-braided my hair and tied the end with matching silk ribbons. Mela wore a green-and-white velvet dress that had once belonged to me. I combed Mela's hair into a ponytail and tied it with green-and-white candy-striped ribbons.

"Mela, you look so festive, and with that ribbon, someone might mistake you for a candy and gobble you up," I said.

"No, they won't."

"They might, you never know," I said, as I buckled her shoes.

"Daddy, Seema says someone will *obble* me up," Mela said. It was amazing how quickly even Mela was picking up English, from watching *Sesame Street* and from her preschool.

"And why would they do such a terrible thing?" he said, suppressing his laughter.

"Because I look like a candy," she said. Her round cheeks were so puffed up that she looked like a hen to me, and I was about to tease her more when Pappa said, "Seema, go help Mommy or else I'll obble *you* up." He could barely finish his sentence, he was trying so hard not to laugh.

"Yes, Dad, right away, sir," I said, and marched upstairs. Then I peeked through the banister and said, "Excuse me, but I forgot to tell you, you look very nice, sir."

His laughter followed me up the stairs. He was dressed up in a light-blue shirt, a leaf-patterned tie that I had picked out for him, and a navy blue sports jacket with beige trousers. He never dressed up when he went to work except on the special days when he had to give a presentation. Today he took extra care.

When I looked in Mommy's room, she was draping her

sari. It was a magenta silk sari with gold and off-white chrysanthemums. It was a perfect fall sari.

"Mom, you'll have to teach me how to wrap a sari," I said.

"Yes. I will."

"You put it on so quickly and smoothly. How does it stay?"

"It stays because I'm used to it. The first few times it kept coming apart, but the more I wore it, the easier it became."

"In India you used to wear saris all the time. How come you don't wear them here every day?"

"We're in Iowa City and not in India," she said. "We get used to what we're surrounded by. Have you noticed how Mela calls Pappa 'Daddy' now? And you call us Mom and Dad sometimes."

"I do?"

"Yes. And we are all getting comfortable speaking in English."

"But I don't want us to forget Gujarati," I said. "If we do, then how would we talk to Dadima? She doesn't know English."

"You won't forget Gujarati," she promised. "I'll make sure of that."

"How about wearing a pearl necklace instead of a gold one?" Pappa suggested when he saw Mommy.

"Why? Doesn't this match?" she asked.

"I think pearls would be better."

This was the first time Pappa had ever commented on something Mommy was wearing. I unclasped her gold necklace with the swastika design. The gold matched her fall sari, and I wondered why Pappa had asked her to wear the pearls instead. Then I remembered from my history class that the swastika we used in India—in our homes, textiles, temples, and jewelry—was feared and despised elsewhere as a symbol of Nazism. That must be the reason why, I decided.

On the way to the Davises' house I thought about how fast everything was changing.

Dr. and Mrs. Davis's house was nestled among the oaks and pines near the Iowa River. The brick exterior reminded me of my school building in India. Mrs. Davis opened the door. She was a large woman with a halo of hair around her face. Her lips were thin and bright red. It made me think of Dadima's saying, "Like the old mare with the red rein," an expression she used when she thought something was inappropriate for her to wear because she was not young anymore. The fire was roaring in the fireplace and there were ten other people in the living room. They were either students of Dr. Davis or his colleagues, and there was no one my age.

When we sat down for dinner I whispered, "I've never seen a table so beautiful,"

"Neither have I," Mommy replied.

The guests were all seated in their chairs and waiting for Mrs. Davis. She brought in a silver platter with a turkey on it. Mela asked in Gujarati, "Daddy, what's that?"

He didn't answer her. Mrs. Davis put the platter on the table. "What's that thing on the table? I don't want to eat that," Mela whispered to me.

"You don't have to," I said.

Everyone was admiring the turkey except us. Dr. Davis carved the turkey, and even though part of me didn't want to look at it, part of me wanted to watch him slice it. I wondered if Mom, Dad, and Mela were feeling the same way. All my family, in fact all the people we knew in India, were vegetarian, so Mela had never eaten turkey or any other meat before. I had seen two aisles at the supermarket filled with meat, but we always skipped those aisles. At school I knew people who brought chicken or tuna sandwiches, but this was the first time I had seen the whole cooked bird sitting on a platter. For the past few weeks when I'd seen turkey advertised on a television show I looked away, but now it was only two feet away from me. I wondered where its head was.

Besides turkey, there were mashed potatoes, green beans, cranberry sauce, three different kinds of rolls and breads, and several different kinds of cheese, so we had plenty to eat. I wished Mrs. Davis hadn't kept apologizing for not having enough food for us and offering us more mashed potatoes and string beans. If I have to eat one more string bean or one more bite of mashed potatoes I am going to throw up, I thought.

The best part of the dinner was all the desserts. The pumpkin pie with cinnamon and nutmeg topped with whipped cream reminded me of an Indian dessert.

On the way home Mela asked, "What was that thing on the plate?"

"Turkey," I said.

"That wasn't a turkey. I have a picture of a turkey. It didn't look like that," she said.

"That's what it was," Mommy said.

"Where was its face?"

"I was wondering the same thing," I said.

On the fifth of December Mela turned five. For her birthday, Mela took treats for her class and invited Mrs. Milan for dinner. Mommy wanted to cook an Indian dinner, but Mela wanted pizza and cake, so that's what we had.

In early December we went on a class trip. On the way back when we stopped for a snack, Sam Bally said, "Hey, Seema, my mom packed an extra can of root beer. Do you want it?"

"I don't drink beer," I said.

"I don't either. This is *root* beer."

"A beer is a beer. I don't want it."

"Okay," he said and popped open his can.

"Danny, want some root beer? Seema here doesn't want to drink it. She doesn't drink any kind of beer," Sam said.

"Why? Don't you like root beer?" Danny asked, opening his can and taking a big gulp.

"I've never had it."

"Why not?"

I didn't know what to think! Sam and Danny were both chugging their root beer. Sam's mom had packed it, so maybe it wasn't *beer*.

"Try a sip," Danny said. "You'll like it."

I took a sip and wished I hadn't. The brown liquid had a medicinal taste and I was sure that it was something I shouldn't have had.

"I guess you didn't like it. I shouldn't have made you try it," Danny said.

All the way back in the bus my mind was filled with the taste of root beer and my heart was filled with fear of how I was going to tell Pappa and Mommy that I had tried something that I shouldn't have.

When we got back to school I told Ria and Jennifer what had happened. Ria began to laugh. Jennifer shot her a look, and suddenly Ria stopped.

"It's all right, Seema. Root beer isn't really beer," Jennifer said.

"It isn't? Then why don't they call it a root drink?"

"Root drink? If they called it a root drink do you think anyone would drink it?" Ria asked.

"I would rather drink something called a root drink then root beer," I said.

That evening when I told Mommy and Pappa what had happened, Mela was listening quietly. At the end I said, "I don't like root beer and I know none of you would either, so we never have to buy it."

Mela said, "I like root beer. It's yummy."

"You never had a root beer," I said.

"Yes, three times," she said raising three fingers.

"Where?"

"At school. Once we had it with ice cream. A root-beer float."

I had no idea what a root-beer float was, but I didn't say anything. The transition from India to America was so different for Mela and me. For her it was as smooth as slipping a pillowcase over a pillow, and for me it was as difficult as turning a cotton pillow into a goose-feather pillow.

One day after school Ria and Jennifer came home with me. They gabbed about Christmas all the way. The last time I had gone to the mall I'd seen trees with pretty things hanging from them.

"We always get a pine tree for Christmas. It smells so good," Ria said.

"We go to the tree lot and my dad cuts the one that has the best shape," Jennifer said.

"You put a real tree in the house?" I asked.

"Yes. Didn't you know that?" Ria asked.

"I didn't," I said, stealing a look at Jennifer.

"It's a little like your Diwali. Tell Ria about the leaves and flowers you hang at Diwali," Jennifer said.

"What's Diwali?" Ria asked.

"Diwali is our biggest holiday. During Diwali we take mango leaves and string them together with yellow marigolds and hang them in our doorways. I remember that special smell of mango leaves and marigold blossoms."

"Marigolds and mango—I can imagine them smelling good together. You can't get mango leaves here, can you?" Ria asked.

"I haven't seen mango trees here," I said. "Come to think of it, I haven't seen *asopalav, neem*, guava, or tamarind trees either."

"Next year on Diwali we can string yellow and red maple leaves," Jennifer suggested.

"It's not the same, but maybe with marigolds they would look pretty," I said.

"And smell good," said Ria.

We walked silently for a while.

"I can't wait to go see my grandparents. They always have snow for Christmas. I also get to see my brand-new cousin who's only ten days old," Ria said.

Jennifer looked over at me and smiled. She knew that all our talk reminded me of my family and our festivals.

Mommy was shelling a pomegranate when we got home.

"What's that?" Ria asked.

"A pomegranate," I said.

"What's a pomegranate?"

"It's a fruit. You've never had it?" I asked.

"No."

Ria and Jennifer tried pomegranate for the first time. "It's . . . it's like having mini juice pockets pop open in your mouth," Ria said, laughing.

Jennifer didn't like it as much. "I like its color. Now I know why in some catalogues they have my favorite shade of red sweaters labeled as pomegranate," she said.

After they went home I thought about how they'd never had pomegranate before and how I'd never seen a live Christmas tree in anyone's house before.

"Seema, there's going to be a dinner party at the Mehtas'. We're invited," Mommy said the next day as soon as I came home from school.

"I don't want to go."

"There'll be many children there and you'll meet them all. Their daughter Asha is in your school. Remember Pappa gave me a list of Indian people a while ago? I invited a few of the women for lunch today and one of them was Mrs. Mehta. She asked me to bring you and Mela."

"Why didn't you tell me about it?"

"I was going to tell you yesterday, but you were so busy talking about Ria's and Jennifer's Christmas plans."

"I'm sorry, Mom."

That night I thought about how every day, as soon as I got home I talked about my day and never asked Mommy about hers. If Mela interrupted I got mad at her. It wasn't right. I made up my mind to listen to Mommy and Mela more.

That Saturday we went to the Mehtas' house. I dressed up in a long skirt and top with a matching sheer scarf. My outfit was pomegranate red with white-beaded embroidery. The embroidery reminded me of Mukta's handkerchief, and I took it out of the drawer and looked at it. I promised myself I'd write her a letter the next day.

The familiar smell of ginger, red pepper, cumin, and turmeric wafted through the air as soon as we entered Mrs. Mehta's house. The music from the movie *Aradhana* was playing in the background, and most of the women were dressed in saris.

Mommy had been right about the children. There were four other girls my age, and two of them went to my school. I'd seen them before. One was Asha and the other was Priya. They talked in American English and I was ashamed of having an accent, but they were so friendly that I soon forgot about it.

All the Indian children in America called adults "Uncle" and "Auntie," and after one party I had many uncles and aunts. The house was filled with their voices and laughter. Mrs. Mehta, or Supriya Auntie as I called her now, had made so many dishes that there was no room to put potatoes on my plate. I thought of not taking any, but they were so tempting, with their diced red and green pepper and chopped-coriander garnish, that I piled them on top of my rice.

While eating I saw Mommy talking and laughing with the others. Her face was as radiant as if it were washed with moonlight. It made me realize how deeply Mommy had missed our family, our friends, and our home.

It was late when we got home and I got up at eleven the next morning. I had so much homework to finish that I forgot about writing a letter to Mukta.

seVeN

On the first day after the winter break Ms. Wilson introduced us to a new student named Carrie Schuler.

"Carrie is from Chicago," Ms. Wilson said. "She has
lived in many different places throughout the country.
Changing school in the middle of the year is always difficult, so I would like our class to welcome Carrie and help
her in any way we can."

I turned around to look at Carrie. Her hair was the
color of chick pea, shiny and smooth, cascading down her
back.

That day when I answered Ms. Wilson I felt a pair of
eyes watching me. I could tell it was Carrie. When I looked
at her, though, her chin was resting on her hand and her

head was down. Like me, she was new to school and I wondered if we could be friends.

At lunch I watched Carrie as she strode toward the cafeteria. She crossed the cafeteria as if she were in her own garden. Before she sat down to eat she looked around and ran her hand through her hair. She was not timid. She was not scared. It was her first day of school and yet she acted as if she knew everyone was going to pay attention to her. When I started my first day of school I kept my gaze down and my hands clasped. Yet here was Carrie breezing into the cafeteria, ready to blow us away with a puff. I admired her and envied her.

Opening my lunch bag, I pointed Carrie out to Jennifer and Ria. "She's so pretty," said Ria.

"Look at her hair. So bouncy and playful," I said.

"Her hair is pretty, but I saw her when she walked in. She walks with an attitude," Jennifer said. Yet all through lunch Jennifer kept watching Carrie. I wondered why.

That evening, I wrote Raju a letter.

Dear Raju,

You can't imagine how cold it gets here! Yesterday I was wearing seventeen things when I walked to school. Even then my hands were cold and stiff and my pen didn't work because the ink was frozen too.

My nose gets so cold that it turns as red as if someone had rubbed hot chili powder on it. I remember when we went to school on Saturday mornings in winter, sometimes we saw our breath. Here I see my breath every day! It's so cold, there isn't a Gujarati word to describe it.

This morning when I woke up it looked like a fairyland. Snow covered everything—roofs, streets, trees, grass, and lampposts. Snow hangs on the evergreen trees and when the sun shines on them I'm reminded of the stories Dadima used to tell us about Lord Shiva on Mount Kailash in the Himalayas.

Like a cat, snow is quiet, except when there's a blizzard. Then the snow swirls and swooshes, the wind howls and shrieks, and the wall of white dances around. I like blizzards and I think you'd like them too.

Some snow is powdery and dry and falls apart when you try to gather it. Some snow is wet and you can gather it up like a ball of rotli dough and throw it around. Jennifer, Ria, and I made a big snowman in front of our house. I stuck a pomegranate on him for a nose. Since I can't mail you a packet of snow, I will take a picture of him and mail it to you with my next letter.

I'm doing better in school now. At least I can

understand what Ms. Wilson is saying. I take English as a second language (ESL) and that's helped me a lot. I think you would've picked up English much faster. Ria and Jennifer are my best friends here, and I met two more girls named Asha and Priya at a party.

Since coming here I realize how many more holidays we have in India. They don't celebrate Uttarayan here. I know you'll enjoy your day off and have lots of fun flying kites and eating sweet tal-sankali. When you write, tell me how much money you find in it. Mommy bought some sesame seeds and brown sugar to make tal-sankali at home. I hope she doesn't forget to put some coins in it. I wonder who's going to help you in kite flying this year? I wish I could be there. Good luck with kite fighting; I hope you win every time and that your kite keeps soaring higher and higher. Make sure you get the sharpest string possible from Paresh Patangwala's store. Harish Manjavala cheats; he shows one string, but sells you another. Don't forget to protect your own hand.

How's everyone at home? I still haven't written to Mukta. If you see her, tell her I'll write her soon.

I'll be thinking about you on the fourteenth of January. Remember last year you picked the first kite,

*and this year it's my turn to pick. Even though I'm not
there, I'm going to pick a red kite. Fly the brightest
red kite that you can find for me.*

 Love,

 Seema

 *P.S. I have bought a map for you and when I visit
I'll bring it with me. There are so many places on it
that I want to show you and tell you about.*

Often, I thought about writing to Mukta, but I was
afraid to ask her about her *kaki*. One more month passed.
The February days were cold, but getting longer. On most
weekends we met Indian families for dinner. The food,
music, and talk made us all happy.

I got to know Asha well, since Asha's mother, Supriya
Auntie, and my mommy became good friends, and her
four-year-old brother Vishal and Mela enjoyed playing
with each other. Many days after school Mommy, Mela,
and I went to their house. When Asha practiced her piano
I watched her hands glide smoothly over the keys. I wished
I could learn to play music like that, but I knew piano lessons were too expensive. In India if I wanted to learn
something I wouldn't have worried about money. Things
were different now. I knew that Mommy and Pappa were
saving money so we could go back to visit India in two

years, and that I had to forget piano lessons if I wanted to visit my family.

In social studies class Ms. Wilson assigned us to present a report on a famous person. We had to research the person and then dress up like him or her and give a three-minute speech. The English and social studies classes were still giving me trouble, and I was terrified about standing up in front of the class and talking for so long.

At lunch one day I talked to Jennifer and Ria about it. Ria said, "You could be Abigail Adams or Sacajawea."

"I don't know who Saca . . . Sacawea is."

"It's not Sacawea, it's Sacajawea," she replied.

Carrie was sitting at the next table and I knew she was listening to our conversation.

"I don't know anything about them. What if I pick a famous Indian person?" I asked softly.

"Who?" Jennifer asked.

"Kasturba Gandhi. She was Mahatma Gandhi's wife."

Ria and Jennifer both nodded.

When I went home I told Mommy that I was going to be Kasturba Gandhi. I had played Kasturba's part the year before in a play, and I knew how she'd marched alongside her husband to gain freedom for India. I knew that the British government had repeatedly thrown her in jail, and yet how strong she'd remained, inspiring a generation of women to fight for freedom. For the part, I'd worn a *khadi* sari, a rough, hand-spun cotton sari like the one Kasturba used to wear.

"I wish I had packed that sari, Mom," I said.

"Which one?" she asked.

"Dadima's *khadi* sari. The one I wore in the play last year."

"Mommy has lots of saris. Why don't you wear her pink sari? It's so pretty," Mela said, coloring a horse crimson.

"Because Kasturba wore only white saris made from the material she wove herself. Isn't that right, Mom?" I said. I turned to look at her, but she was gone.

"I don't like white saris," Mela said.

"Then you shouldn't be Kasturba."

Mommy returned with the sari that I'd worn for the play. "You packed it?" I was astonished.

"Dadima asked me to take it for you. I really didn't want to carry it, but she said, 'It is Seema's special sari and you had better take it.' I must say that I almost took it out of the suitcase at the last minute when I couldn't fit all the things we wanted to bring here."

"What made you bring it?"

"When Dadima told me that she'd helped weave this sari when she was ten years old, it became too precious. I had to bring it."

"I'm so glad!"

Over the next few days, I wrote my speech. Mommy and Pappa both read it. I memorized it. I tried putting on my sari a few times until I could do it without Mommy's help. Now I needed the courage to get up in the front of the class in that sari and say my speech.

I'd noticed that whenever I spoke in class, Carrie watched me intently. Whenever I left to go to my math class, I felt her eyes glued to my back and it made me uneasy, because she never spoke to me. One day at lunch she sat next to me. There was not enough room, so I slid closer to Ria. Carrie didn't say thank you or give me a smile.

"My name is Carrie and I come from Lakeshore School. It's a private school," she announced.

"I'm Jennifer and this is Ria and this is See—"

"Hi, Jennifer. Hi, Ria. Nice to meet you," Carrie interrupted.

"Aren't you in Seema's class?" Ria asked.

"Yes," Carrie said.

"Hi, Carrie," I said.

"Hi," she replied, with the warmth of freezing drizzle.

Jennifer glanced at me. I shrugged my shoulders.

"How do you like our school?" Ria asked.

"I'm in a dumb class and I'm bored. Some people don't

even know how to speak English. In my old school people like that would never get admitted," Carrie said, shooting a glance at me.

I felt the blood rushing to my face. Through my wheat-colored skin they would never know how embarrassed and mad I was, so I was safe. I began eating my sandwich faster.

"Seema is in algebra. Maybe you can take that. It'll be challenging," said Jennifer.

"Very challenging," Ria said, and nudged me with her elbow.

"I don't know if I have the time to take on extra work."

"It's not extra work," I said.

"Not extra, just more difficult," Jennifer said.

"I'll see," Carrie mumbled. Her face had lost its luster.

"Seema, have you figured out what you're going to be for social studies class?" Ria asked.

"Yes. Didn't I tell you? I'm going to be Kasturba, Mah——"

"Who is Kastur——whatever the name is? No one on this planet knows who that is," Carrie said.

"Kasturba was Mahatma Gandhi's wife, and millions of people in India and the world over know about her," I said.

Before Carrie could say anything I took the last gulp of my juice and got up saying, "Bye, Jennifer. Bye, Ria. See you later."

I don't know what happened after I left, but that afternoon Carrie glared at me. Her hair that I had thought was so pretty when she first came to school now looked like a thousand glassy-eyed lizards.

That afternoon as I was getting my things ready for algebra class, Carrie wrote something on a piece of paper and passed it to the next desk. Sam picked up the paper, read it, and laughed. Then Danny read it and giggled. Just as he was passing the note back to Carrie, I grabbed it and walked out. It read, *It seems that Seema can't seem to learn English. Give Seema some math and she seems to be satisfied.*

I didn't know what to do with the note. When I first started school I had been so worried about not knowing English, but Ms. Wilson had helped me and so had my ESL teacher. After six months of school, when I was feeling so much more comfortable, Carrie had to come and spoil it all. I wished Jennifer or Ria were in my class. I wouldn't be alone then. If Raju were here, it would be even better.

At dinner Mela tilted her head and asked sweetly, "You look sad, Seema. Are you hurting?"

I began to cry. Even though Mommy had made my favorite meal, spicy bread and potatoes cooked with tomato gravy, I couldn't eat.

I told Mommy that I was worried about Carrie. She listened to me and tried to comfort me. "Tomorrow will be better."

"How do you know?"

"I don't. You have to believe that, though."

Instead of the next day being better it turned out to be the worst day yet.

"If Carrie weren't in my class I wouldn't be so nervous about the presentation," I confessed at breakfast.

"She's only one person and she can't do anything to you. You have to draw your courage from who you are. After all, you're going to be Kasturba and you're going to wear a sari that Dadima wove. Think of all those brave women who fought for independence," Mommy said.

I repeated Mommy's words to myself as if it they were a magical mantra. I was so afraid of Carrie that I worried that fear would dry my mouth and I wouldn't be able to get a word out. I chewed nervously on the end of my pencil when social studies began. Danny was the first to present. He was the Green Bay Packers' quarterback, Brett Favre. Dressed in a green jersey with the number four on it, a helmet and shoulder pads, he looked like a mini version of the players I'd seen on TV. I didn't understand American football, so I didn't know what he was talking about. When I watched football, unlike with cricket, I couldn't see the ball, and every play ended with men piling up on one another. Many kids asked Danny questions, so it took a long time for him to finish. After Danny, Kim talked about Sally Ride, the first woman astronaut to travel into space. By that time my stomach began to twirl. I put my arm on it to hold it in place.

When I was two kids away from presenting, the bell rang and Ms. Wilson said that the rest of us would have to present the next day.

Carrie turned to Danny and said, "I don't like Brett Favre, because I'm a Bears fan, but I liked your speech. It was the best."

"Thanks," he said.

"I wish we were done already. Tomorrow will be *so* boring. We should have a rule to only present people we know. Who cares about a bunch of strange people from some foreign country?"

Danny didn't answer her. She went on, "Don't be surprised if I call in sick tomorrow or if I *s-e-e-m* to get sick just before someone's presentation." She stretched out the "seem" so long that Danny gave me a quick glance. This fueled Carrie. "You seem to know what I am saying. Maybe I'll show up. It'll be fun!" she snickered.

I got up to leave for my ESL class.

"Good luck getting rid of your accent, Seem-a," Carrie pressed each sound as if she were sipping a delicious drink.

I stopped. Say something, I urged myself, anything. But nothing came to my lips.

She laughed. I don't know if anyone laughed with her. I fled.

All through English I was too upset to learn a word. As soon as the bell rang I left without waiting for Jennifer or Ria. I had a problem and had to work it out myself.

It had snowed about an inch that afternoon, which made the sidewalks slick. I was still not used to walking very fast on snow, and suddenly, someone tugged my braid. As I turned to look I lost my balance, slid, and fell flat on my back. My right elbow was scraped and my right hand hurt, but I managed to get up. When I looked back all I saw were the masses of chick-pea—colored hair bouncing away.

Mommy bandaged my elbow and rubbed some almond oil on my hand. She didn't ask how I fell and I didn't tell her, not until that night, after Mela went to bed. "Mom, can you listen to my speech one more time?" I asked.

"Yes," she said.

"You've done good work," she said when I'd finished.

"Thanks," I said, looking away from her.

"Seema, why are you so upset?"

All evening long I'd been thinking about Carrie.

"I don't want to go to school tomorrow."

"Why? What's the matter? Your speech is perfect, and now you wrap your sari as well as I do."

"It's Carrie . . ." I began and told her about my whole day.

"Are you sure she pulled your braid?"

"I think so," I said. "No one else would do that."

"Why would she do such a thing?"

"Mom, that's how she is. You don't know her. You don't have to go to school with her," I said.

"Even if she's unpleasant, remember what Dadima used to say."

"What did Dadima used to say?" I asked.

"That an unpleasant person is like a tiny boil. If you keep thinking about it and keep feeling it with your hands it gets bigger and bigger. The best way to get rid of it is to ignore it."

"She's in my class. There's no way to ignore her," I said.

"Do you want me to talk to Ms. Wilson?"

"No." I didn't want Mommy to come and talk to Ms. Wilson. "*Padeshe ava devashe*, I'll deal as it comes. I'll be fine," I mumbled.

"By the way, this came for you today," Mommy said, handing me an envelope.

Before I saw the sender's name I knew by the oil spots that it was from Mukta.

Dear Seema,

You must've received my letter because Raju gave me your message that you would write me a letter soon. Every day I wait for it and wonder if it got lost in the mail. School is going all right for me. I am not doing that good because I have no time to study. Since Kaki is sick Mommy and I take care of my little cousin and keep him and my sister away from Kaki as much as possible.

In the last two weeks Mommy and I have been making flower garlands for the temples. Since I help the tailor in the shop next to us, I've learned to be quick with needles and thread, and I like to work with flowers. Every day we get a basketful of roses, jasmine, chrysanthemums, and marigolds. When I sit next to the baskets and make garlands I don't smell the smoke of Pappa and Kaka frying snacks. When the fragrance of roses fills our house, I imagine that our home is a garden. We have planted a rose in an empty oil can, but I don't know when it will bloom.

All the garland-making work leaves me no time for studies, but we're making good money so we can send Kaki to a sanitarium for a rest. Kaka is taking her there next week. I hope she comes back healthy.

How's school for you? Have you made a friend in your class? Is Iowa City as big as Vishanagar, or

*smaller? I heard Raju saying to someone that you have
your own room. Is that true? Do you walk to school?
Does everyone have a car? Do roses and jasmine
grow there?*

Say hello to your family. Write soon.

Mukta

Trouble is like the head of the cobra, always looking
bigger and scarier than it really is. Like Mukta, I have to
be brave and capture the cobra and make it dance, I
thought as I finished reading her letter.

I reread Mukta's letter, folded it, and slipped it in my
backpack with my speech and my sari.

Courage was with me.

eight

Wearing my white sari, I stood up to give my speech. My mouth felt as dry as a shriveled-up date. I wondered how I'd be able to speak, and I wished there was something I could clutch. But there was nothing there to support me except the eager faces of the other students.

I knitted my fingers together and began.

"I was born on April 11, 1869, at Porbandar, Gujarat. My name is Kasturba Gandhi. When I was only thirteen, I married Mohandas Gandhi, who was six months younger than me. Out of respect people called him Gandhiji."

The first few sentences had spilled from my mouth as if I'd had no control over them. I paused, took a deep breath, and looked at Danny. He had his hands on his chin and his eyes on my face. He smiled. I continued, "My husband taught me to read and write. In 1888, while I stayed back in India with our son, Harilal, Gandhiji sailed to England to become a lawyer. After finishing his studies, he came back to India and set up his practice. A few years later he went to South Africa to fight a case. Within days of his arrival, when traveling by first class, he was thrown off a train, assaulted by a white coachman, and pushed off a sidewalk—all because of his color. He saw firsthand how badly the Africans were treated by their white rulers, and he learned how Indian laborers were forced to work under semislave conditions."

My words had begun to flow more smoothly now. I glanced at Ms. Wilson standing on the right side of the room, and she gave me a slight nod.

"Gandhiji came back to India in 1896. By then we'd had another son and we all sailed to Durban, South Africa together. During the long voyage Gandhiji told me many stories, and taught me history and geography as we watched the night sky together.

"In South Africa, Gandhiji and I set up a place for communal living and began a simple life like the poor people of South Africa.

"Gandhiji promoted the principle of *satyagraha*—an active but nonviolent defiance against injustice. It was a technique that required fearlessness, sacrifice, and suffering. I did not always agree with Gandhiji. Although we argued over some of his ideas, *satyagraha* was one I believed in. I led the women's *satyagraha* in South Africa, and for that I was arrested and sentenced to three months' hard labor.

"In jail I had to wake up at five in the morning and wait in my cell for an hour. The jail food was impossible to eat. For breakfast, I had to eat bland, unsalted soup made of corn flour; for lunch, I had to eat rice and bread; and, for dinner, I had to eat corn soup and potatoes. I was not allowed to have any tea or coffee. When I was released from jail I was frail, but my spirit was strong and solid."

Once again I took a deep breath. I unclasped my hands.

"In 1915 my entire family came back to India, where the British ruled at the time. I worked side by side with my husband for India's independence. Besides showing the path of *satyagraha*, I also taught village women reading, writing, cleanliness, and discipline. Over the years, Gandhiji was arrested many times. In his absence, I gradually became a leader, addressing meetings, collecting funds, and keeping up the morale of the people. I had gone to jail before and I was not afraid."

As I spoke about *satyagraha*, I felt calmer, stronger. I made eye contact with Sam and was surprised to see that he wasn't slouching as usual but sitting up straight.

"With other people we worked for the freedom of our

country. We only wore clothes made of a simple, rough fabric called *khadi* that we'd spun ourselves, like this sari I am wearing today.

"*Khadi* was an important symbol of our struggle, strength, and unity against the unfair British rule. This was because the British took raw cotton from India to England at a very cheap price. After turning the cotton into material in their mills, they sold it back to Indians at an inflated price that the people couldn't afford. We picketed foreign cloth shops, and for that I was jailed. I was released only after Gandhiji went on a prolonged fast in protest of British rule, and he became very frail."

Carrie was sitting in front of me, but so far I'd avoided looking at her. Then something unexpected happened. I looked at her as if she were Sam or Danny or any of the other students. I wasn't afraid of her.

"Over and over again I was thrown in jail for participating in *satyagraha*. On the morning of August 9, 1942, before a very important meeting, Gandhiji and other leaders were arrested. I decided to address the meeting in my husband's place, but on the way I, too, was arrested and sent to the Aga Khan Palace detention camp where he was held. The place was ringed with barbed wire, and armed police guarded it. My health began to fail there, and as the sun set on February 22, 1944, I died in my husband's arms.

"I'd asked Gandhiji to have me cremated in a *khadi* sari that he'd spun. After my death, the Kasturba Gandhi National Memorial Trust was established for the service of simple women like me and their children."

I paused, looked straight at Carrie, and finished my speech. "I still live through the courage and dignity of the women in India and the world over."

The class was silent. I looked at Ms. Wilson. She smiled and began clapping, and so did everyone else. I joined my palms and said *namaste* before walking back to my seat.

NINE

On Saturday I read Mukta's letter over and over again. I was desperate to talk to someone about Mukta, and in the afternoon when Ria and Jennifer came over, Mukta's letter whirled in my head. I wanted to tell them about her, but how could I explain Mukta to them?

I could tell them about how poor Mukta was or how her clothes smelled or how her aunt was sick with tuberculosis. I could tell them about the garden in the container that she'd grown, the handkerchief she'd made for me. I could tell them about the sweetness of Mukta's mother's voice, and about Mukta's determination to continue her studies and help her *kaki*. But how could I explain how Mukta had taught me courage and kindness when I'd showed her none? It was the feel of Mukta in my heart that would be hard to explain. So I didn't say a word about her to Jennifer or Ria.

That evening we were invited to Asha's house for dinner. As I listened to Asha playing piano I realized it would be just as hard to tell Asha about Mukta as it would be to tell Jennifer and Ria. Asha's parents were from India, but she was born and raised in Iowa City, and the last time she had visited India she was only six years old. I didn't think she would understand about Mukta. There was something that separated us. Like a fog, it stretched out between me and everyone else, including my friends. It was because I'd grown up in a different place. When they talked about music, books, or movies I was always the outsider listening in, not comprehending their conversation completely and never participating in it. I realized how Mukta might have felt when we were too busy with our circle of friends, talking about the vacation we were going to take, or the new clothes we were getting for Diwali, or the birthday celebration we were planning. That was not her world and she must have felt different from us.

At night when Mommy came to say good night I took her hand in mine and said, "Don't go. Sit."

"It's late and I'm tired and sle——" before she finished her sentence she saw the look in my eyes. "What is it, Seema?"

"It's Mukta. I'm afraid she won't be able to study

anymore. I keep thinking about her. Urvashi, Nalini, and Anita, none of them have written more than one letter, only Mukta has. And it's not easy for her to write. She doesn't have time or money. The postage is expensive, isn't it?"

"Yes. Have you written to her?"

I didn't answer.

I told Mommy about Mukta's letter. She was quiet. "I want to write to her, but I don't know what to say. Our lives are so different," I said.

"Friendship does not happen because you have the same lifestyle; neither does it depend on it. You should answer Mukta's letter."

"What can I say?"

"Start writing and it will come."

"Yes. I guess so," I said.

On Sunday I wrote Mukta a letter.

Dear Mukta,

This letter has been on my mind for a long time and I should have written it long ago. I hope all of you are doing well, including your kaki. By the time you get this letter she will probably be in the sanitarium. Mommy said that one of her kakas had tuberculosis and he went to the Jitheri Sanitarium for three months. He got better and he now lives in

Palitana with his family. He's 77 years old. Do you know which sanitarium your kaki *is going to?*

How is the garland-making going? Whenever I bought a garland I never thought about who made it. I'm glad that you've found work and are able to help your kaki. *I hope you continue your studies.*

Sometimes it is hard for me to keep up my studies here too. Everything is so different: the school, the way they teach, and even the weather, which makes going and coming back hard. Imagine me bundled up like a bale of cotton and walking down a snowy, slippery sidewalk.

English and history are the hardest subjects for me. You would enjoy history here, because there are so many books for children to read from and some of them are like storybooks or small novels. Whenever I look at them I think of you.

Most families have cars here. And I do have my own room, but only for this year, because next year we will live in an apartment and it will be much smaller than this house.

It is winter here and the garden is covered with snow. I wish I could have a basketful of roses and jasmine. There are shops here that sell flowers all year round. I've seen roses there, but never any jasmine. They get their flowers from far away, so they're expensive and we don't buy them.

I hope your sister and cousin are doing well. Say hello to your family for me.

I signed the letter *Seema*, then I changed my mind and wrote, *Your friend, Seema.*

Once I had written the letter I felt better and wished I had done it earlier. A week passed and I found myself anxiously waiting for Mukta's letter. Even if she replied right away I knew it would be a month before I received an answer from her, but that didn't stop me from waiting.

In school Carrie and I had a relationship like two icicles: cold, sharp, and slippery. I stayed away from her as much as I could, but being in the same class it was impossible to avoid her completely, and a little spat occasionally occurred. Some days I wished that the first few months of school would come back when I didn't have Carrie to worry about, but time once gone is gone forever. I knew I couldn't bring it back.

One day I took cauliflower and potatoes rolled up in *rotli* for lunch. I was getting tired of sandwiches, and besides, Asha and Priya told me they took Indian food for lunch all the time. That day Jennifer was sick and only Ria and I were sitting together. When I'd eaten more than half of my roll-up Carrie walked over from the bench across from me and said, "I wish you wouldn't bring such smelly lunches. It ruins my appetite."

"I will bring whatever I want to eat. If you don't like it, wear a mask," I said.

"You come to my country and you act like a lord. If you want to live here, eat what we eat and speak the language we speak."

"Except for American Indians, all of us were immigrants once," Ria said.

"Yes, but we were here first," Carrie said.

"Are you saying whoever came first rules?" I said.

"Yes."

"Well, I came to this school before you did, so I rule."

"That's right," Ria said.

"You seem to think your friend Seema is great, but I disagree. Seema's a strange name and she's a strange creature."

"You know what you are to me, Carrie Schuler?"

"What?" she said.

"*Schuler* means 'pain' in my language, and you are a big pain to me," I said.

"*Schuler* means 'pain'?" Danny asked. He was sitting behind me.

I turned to him and whispered, "Sort of."

When I turned back Carrie was gone.

The next day I told Jennifer all about it. "I'm glad you told her off," she said.

"Now I hope she leaves me alone. I don't want to turn nasty like her," I said.

A few days after the outburst, we had spring break and I enjoyed a week free of Carrie.

When March was almost over the days became longer, the sun shone brighter, and the southerly winds blew warmer. The snow was disappearing fast. In India I had not known the difference between the length of summer and winter days, which only changed by an hour at the most. On a sunny afternoon I saw many people outdoors like columns of ants descending on crystals of spilled sugar. Where had they been all winter long?

Flowers with unfamiliar names were blooming in the garden. Before Mrs. Milan left to visit relatives in Georgia, she came over to tell us all about the flowers. The first ones to bloom were crocuses. The yellow and the white ones were narcissus. In a few days she said that the tulips would begin to bloom.

One day I noticed that the fragrance of jasmine perfumed the air. I looked for a white or yellow bloom of jasmine, but couldn't find any. Instead, I spotted a stalk with a cluster of blue blossoms that filled the garden with its delicate scent. "Mom, what is this flower called?" I asked.

"I don't know. It's so sweet smelling," she said,

closing her eyes and breathing in the fragrance.

"Maybe it's jasmine. Blue jasmine," I said.

"I've never heard of blue jasmine."

"You'd never heard of crocuses and narcissus before either."

"That's true," she said.

"I'm going to call it blue jasmine," I said.

When Mrs. Milan came back she told me that the blue jasmine was not jasmine but hyacinth. "Hyacinth is a flower of the lily family and jasmine is a flower of the olive family," she said.

"Are they quite different?"

"Yes, they are."

"They have similar scents."

"I never thought of that, but they do," she agreed.

More and more flowers bloomed, and the names of those flowers were so hard to remember that I made Mrs. Milan write them down. Next to their names she drew pictures of them. I liked all of them, but my favorite was the blue hyacinth, because of its special color and familiar fragrance. In India, I had only seen a poster of a blue flower called the Himalayan poppy, but no blue flower bloomed in our garden. And yet the blue hyacinths were fragrant like jasmine, so I took a picture of them and mailed it to Raju.

I thought of Mukta and the basketful of flowers. I

wondered what she would think of my garden full of flowers.

On my way to school, I noticed that the gray house on the corner had a SOLD sign on it, and I wondered who might be moving. As I turned the corner I saw that the park was blanketed with yellow flowers, as if someone had sprinkled turmeric on the lawn. I admired the flowers fluttering in the breeze before I realized that I was late. I picked two of the flowers, put them in my hair, and hurried toward school.

As soon as I got to school the first bell rang and I rushed to my classroom without seeing Jennifer or Ria. If only I had seen them! When I sat down I heard Carrie's whisper followed by a wave of laughter. The entire class was snickering and suppressing giggles. I turned around. Carrie winked at me and said, "Nice flowers."

"Thank you," I said. I didn't understand what was so funny about putting flowers in my hair. In the social studies classroom there were picture of Hawaiian girls wearing hibiscus and plumeria in their hair.

At lunch Ria and Jennifer were already sitting down to eat when I got there. "Seema, why have you stuck dandelions in your hair?" Ria said, pointing at the flowers.

"These were blooming in the park, and they looked so

pretty. There were hundreds, maybe thousands of them, and I picked two. Maybe I shouldn't have done that. Is it against the law to pick—"

"Don't worry about the law. These are weeds. Do you know what weeds are? People yank them out and throw them away. Nobody wants them in their yard, let alone in their hair," Ria said.

Jennifer couldn't wait any longer. She plucked the flowers from my hair and slid them in her empty brown bag. To me they still looked pretty. I fought back my tears. Now I knew why Carrie had complimented me. Now I understood why all the students were smirking and giggling. Just when I thought I knew English well, just when I was starting to feel more at home, I did something stupid and messed it all up. For the first time in a long time I felt like running away from school, from Iowa City, back to my old school, back to Raju and Vishanagar.

I couldn't remember what we learned that afternoon. When I came home Mommy asked, "Don't you want a snack?"

"I'm not hungry. Can I go over to Mrs. Milan's?" I asked, and was almost out the door before Mommy said, "Can you take Mela, please? I want to start cooking dinner."

I swung back, grabbed Mela's hand, and took off.

When Mrs. Milan opened the door she said, "My, my, we are in a big hurry today!"

She saw the distraught look on my face.

"Sweet pea, didn't I see you walking home from school only two minutes ago? You must have dropped off your backpack, grabbed your sister, and rushed right over here."

"I did," I confessed. "I have a question to ask you. Why does everyone hate dandelions? I think they're such pretty flowers. They don't smell sweet, but they are so cheerful. I can't understand why people hate them. And why don't girls and women ever wear flowers in their hair? In India we used to put flowers in our hair often. It looked . . . I can't explain . . . so pretty."

"Oh, my. You certainly have lot on your mind. Shall we sit down and have cookies and milk and discuss dandelions, Mela?"

"Cookies." Mela clapped her hands.

"You must have seen the park full of dandelions on your way to school."

I nodded, taking a bite out of my butterscotch-oatmeal cookie.

"Aren't they beautiful? Not everyone hates them. I, for one, love dandelion greens in salad."

"You can eat them?"

"Yes. They are a perennial herb. They grow in temperate regions and that's why, like tulips and crocuses, you haven't seen them before. Those pretty yellow flowers are used in making dandelion wine."

"You're pulling my leg," I said.

"No, no. It's the truth. And when I was little my parents couldn't afford real coffee, so they used dandelion roots to make coffee."

"Then why do people hate them?"

"Dandelions are too successful," she said.

"What do you mean?"

"In a few days the pretty yellow flower will turn into white globes of down, and with the wind they will ride far and wide. That's how they spread, and if people don't control them, they take over the lawns."

"I see," I said, wiping Mela's face with a napkin. And that's when I looked out and realized that Mrs. Milan didn't have any lawn in her front yard. She had trees and flowers and meandering brick paths, but no grass. "How come you don't have any lawn?"

"Because I love gardens and hate fighting with dandelions. I don't have an answer to your second question as to why women and girls don't wear flowers in their hair. Maybe it's a cultural thing. Maybe you can tell me why you wear flowers in your hair," she said.

"I . . . I don't know why. We just do . . . did. Maybe because we have so many flowers growing all the time and it looks pretty."

"Did you wear dandelions in your hair today?"

"Yes."

"You left the barn door open with that one," she said.

"I did what?" I asked.

"It's a Southern saying. I grew up in Georgia, and there it means that you made a mistake."

"Then I did leave the barn door wide open with that one," I said.

Later, as I set the table for dinner, I said, "Mom, I feel strange calling Mrs. Milan, Mrs. Milan. It seems so . . . so distant. It reminds me of our gym class in India, when they used to make us stand at attention. Our eyes straight ahead, chin up, chest out, stomach in; we didn't look like kids, we looked like faceless wooden dolls."

"What would you like to call her? Aunt Milan?"

"No, that's not right either. Besides, all the Indian women in this country are my aunts. I have no shortage of them."

Mommy stopped chopping cilantro and touched my cheek with her moist fingers and laughed. "I see. Since we aunts are oversupplied, we're of no value to you. But let me remind you that we don't have a shortage of nieces and nephews, either."

"Mom! I didn't mean it that way. I'm glad to have all the aunts, but Mrs. Milan is older, like Dadima or Nanima. Do you think I can call her Grandma?" I said.

"I suppose so."

"Maybe I should ask her."

"Yes, ask her," Mommy said.

"I will."

ten

Spring started like a soft hum and turned into a beautiful song. *I'm glad my birthday comes in spring*, I wrote in my notebook. In India, I envied Mela, because her birthday came in December. At that time the garden was lush, the sky was azure, and the warm days were twinned with cool nights. My birthday came in May. At that time the garden was dry, the sky was scorching, and the hot days were twinned with muggy nights. Every year on my birthday we prayed for the monsoon to come and bring some relief. Here the month of May had already given me the gift of warm, long days and blooming gardens.

Carrie was sick with chicken pox and had missed two weeks of school. In class, no one teased me, and no one snickered when I mispronounced a word. It was very pleasant without her, and I wished she'd stay away from school permanently.

One day our class made a giant card to send to Carrie. Everyone signed it with a little message. When it was my turn I thought of not signing at all. With the entire class writing, I knew no one would notice that I had skipped it, but I thought that Carrie would probably notice. She would fume and that would delight me. Then I remembered what Dadima used to say to us when Raju, Uma, and I were mean to anyone. She told us, "Show *daya*, compassion, and you will be showered with love." I knew well that Carrie had not a speck of love for me. She was sick, though, and I should do as much as I could to make her feel better. So I wrote, "Carrie, I hope you are getting better every day." Then I drew a blue jasmine and signed my name. That day when I walked home I was glad I'd written and signed the card, because if I hadn't I knew I would have fought with myself. This way it was done and I had nothing to fret about.

The next day Ria told me she'd seen Carrie at the grocery store. "She's coming back on Monday."

"This Monday?" I asked.

"Yes."

"It won't be so bad," Jennifer offered.

I didn't know what to say.

"I hope you're right, Jennifer. Carrie was surprisingly friendly, and she even asked about Seema," Ria said.

"She asked about me? What did she say?"

"They've moved into the gray house and she was wondering if you lived nearby," Ria said.

"Are you sure?" Jennifer asked.

"I hope you're wrong, Ria," I said, shaking my head.

What if Carrie used her time at home to plot against me? She is determined to make me miserable! That sickening thought hung in my mind like a stubborn lizard hanging on the ceiling.

On Saturday Mela begged me to take her to the park. When we reached the park I glanced at the gray house across the street. It looked peaceful, as if no one were home. Mela went up and down the slide ten times and then she climbed up the monkey bars. "Let's swing side by side, Seema," she said, pulling my hand. While Mela and I were swinging I saw Carrie strolling toward us. I wished we weren't on the swings; then we could have marched away. I noticed that Carrie was missing the bounce in her walk, and without it, she seemed different. As I slowed down I saw that she was holding something in her hands.

By the time she reached us I had stopped swinging.

"I picked these flowers for you," she said.

I didn't look at them, but from the corner of my eyes I could see a little yellow and I was certain they were dandelions. "No, thanks," I snapped. "You picked them. You keep them."

"I want them," Mela said as she got off the swing. Carrie gave her the flowers. They were not dandelions. "They are pretty," said Mela. "Thank you."

"Is this your sister?" Carrie asked me.

"Yes." I said gingerly, afraid that she might say something nasty to Mela and make her cry.

"Are you my sister's friend?" Mela asked.

Carrie glanced at me.

"I'm in her class."

"Are these flowers from your garden?"

"They are. I live right across the park," she said, pointing at the gray house.

"What's your name?" Mela asked.

"My name is Carrie."

"I like your name, Carrie. My name is Mela and I'm five."

"Do you want a push, Mela?" Carrie asked.

Mela nodded, handed me the flowers, and hopped back on the swing. Before I could say or do anything Carrie gave Mela a push.

"Your sister is cute. How come she doesn't have an accent like you?" Carrie asked.

"Because she learned English after coming here, but I started learning English in India."

"When did you move here?"

"Last July," I said, wishing she wouldn't ask me any more questions. Who knows how she would use all the information against me in school?

She gave Mela another big push. "Are you coming to my sister's birthday party, Carrie?" Mela shouted from her swing.

"When is your birthday?" Carrie asked.

"Not until the twenty-third."

I didn't know what else to say. One part of me urged me to be polite and invite her. Then I could get even and make fun of her on home territory. Another part of me warned me to shut up. Why invite trouble to my house?

She was about to give Mela another push when I said, "I can do that."

"I don't mind. I forgot, what's your sister's name?"

"Mela."

"My name means 'carnival,'" Mela piped up.

"You're fun like a carnival," Carrie said. "What does your name mean, Seema?"

I remembered how she'd broken my name up into "Seem-a" and ridiculed me in front of the others. I looked away from her. My eyes rested on the park lawn where the last of the dandelions were still blooming while most had turned white, like flower ghosts. Why should I tell you what my name means? I thought, but instead, I said, "Seema means 'boundary,' 'horizon.' "

"That's pretty," she said. Then she smiled.

I almost flipped off the swing. I wondered what evil thoughts were lurking behind her smile. All I wanted to do was to get away from Carrie before she said or did something dreadful to us.

"Mela, time to go home," I said. As we walked away Mela kept looking back waving and shouting, "Bye-bye, Carrie. Bye-bye, Carrie." And Carrie stood by the swing waving and shouting, "Bye-bye, Mela. Bye, Seema."

On the way home Mela asked, "Are you going to invite Carrie to your birthday party?"

"I don't know," I said.

"I like her."

"Then you invite her for your birthday," I snapped.

Mela didn't say another word.

At home I fought with the thought that maybe I should invite Carrie to my birthday party, but memories of all the times she'd been mean tumbled through my mind. She was not my friend and I wasn't going to invite her to my party. Then I realized all my friends, Jennifer, Ria, Asha, and Priya, would be there. Wouldn't it be fun to have one enemy and make her miserable? I liked the idea.

That afternoon I wrote the invitations for my birthday party.

"Can I invite one more person?" I asked Mommy.

"Of course. Who do you want to invite?"

"Mela and I saw Carrie at the park today. I think she'd like to come to my party."

"Do you want to invite her?"

"Yes. I do."

"Then go ahead," Mommy said.

After I dropped the card in the mailbox I worried I'd made a mistake. What if she spoiled my birthday? What if she made fun of my family? But we would be five against one and we'd show her. No matter what happened I had to face her. I've invited her and I have to go through with it, I thought.

Mukta still hadn't answered my letter. When I talked to Raju on the phone I asked him if he had seen her.

"Why would I see stinky Mukta if I didn't have to?" he said.

"Don't call her stinky," I said.

"You used to call her that, too, but now that you're far away and can't smell her, you want to be nice to her."

I wanted to shout at him. Instead, I gulped down my anger and asked calmly, "Does she come to school?"

"If she came to school, she'd be the only one doing that. We're on vacation."

"Oh yeah, I forgot."

"We still have four more weeks of vacation, and when school starts I'll tell you if she shows up, and stinks up."

I couldn't talk to Raju anymore. I handed the phone to Pappa.

Raju's conversation turned my mood so dark that I had a hard time concentrating on my math homework. How could he be so mean to Mukta? But Raju was right. I used to call Mukta stinky too. I remembered when the tip of my pencil broke during a math exam, Mukta offered me one of her tiny pencils, but I wouldn't touch it. Now I was ashamed to realize how that must have hurt Mukta. Only now that I had suffered the pain inflicted by Carrie in her nastiness did I realize the pain I was guilty of inflicting on Mukta.

When I woke up Sunday morning Mommy was listening to a tape. It was in Hindi. Of course this past year I had not learned any more Hindi in school as I would have in India, but I had seen a few Hindi movies.

"Tulsi es sansar me, bhat bhat ke lok
Subse mil-zul chaliye, nadi, nav sanjog."

"Mom, what does Tulsidas's song mean?" I asked.

"It says that in this world there are many kinds of people. To sail smoothly through life, adjust yourself according to circumstances as a boat adjusts to the flow of the river and the wind."

From that moment on, whenever I thought about what I could do to make Carrie miserable, Mukta's face came to mind, and I couldn't think of a single evil prank.

When Jennifer and Ria found out that I had invited Carrie to the party they were shocked. "You're joking! Tell me you're joking!" Ria said.

"I'm not." I said, and told them about the time I had seen Carrie in the park.

Jennifer shook her head. "Seema, I don't understand why you'd do that."

"I don't know myself. First I thought it would be fun to make her miserable, but the more I thought about it the less I wanted revenge. My biggest worry is that she might ruin my party."

"We'll be there. We'll show her," Ria promised.

Jennifer nodded.

In the classroom I noticed that Carrie moved slowly, differently. She was friendlier. It reminded me of a one-actor play I had seen in a village in India. Depending on the role he was playing, the actor changed his looks, voice, walk, and mannerisms. When he went from being a fierce demon to a celestial dancer the audience laughed, but he kept on acting and telling his story. I wondered if

Carrie was acting the role of my friend because I'd invited her to my party. Or was there a genuine change in her? Was it temporary, and as soon as my party was over she'd strike again? Was I missing something that was obvious to everyone but me? I couldn't tell.

Now every time I spoke in class Carrie watched me intently as she used to when she had first arrived, but she didn't snicker and didn't make jokes. A couple of times when I answered correctly I saw from the corner of my eye that she was smiling at me, but I avoided meeting her eyes. Even though she wasn't unpleasant I avoided her as much as I could. One day as I was walking home she caught up with me. "Wait, Seema," she said.

I stopped.

"I'm sorry about that day."

"Which day?" I asked as I started walking. I was thinking that there were so many days that she should be sorry for.

"The day you fell."

"You mean the day you *made* me fall?"

"I barely touched your braid and—"

"You made me fall and then you ran away," I snapped.

"I'm sorry," she mumbled.

I didn't say anything. We were both quiet until we reached the edge of the park.

I knew she had to cross the street. "Thanks for inviting me to your party," she whispered, as she stopped.

I glanced at her, and I thought I saw tears forming in the corners of her eyes.

"Are you coming?" I asked, focusing my eyes on the sky beyond her.

"Yes. I'll be there."

I nodded and walked away.

So it was definitely Carrie who had pulled my braid and run away. On top of being mean, she's a coward, I thought. That mean coward is going to pay. She's going to find out what it's like to be on the receiving end of meanness.

Thoughts of revenge took hold of me.

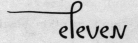 eleven

On my birthday Raju called early in the morning. "Now I'm a teenager," I said to him.

"What's a teenager?"

"I'm thirteen," I said.

"I know. I was with you for your first twelve birthdays, remember? But what's a teenager?"

I tried to explain. "When you turn thirteen until you're nineteen there's a *teen* in the number."

"I see. But what's the big deal?"

"No big deal," I said. Some things were hard to explain; others were impossible.

"There's a card for you in the mail," Pappa said.

One of the stamps had pictures of Mahatma Gandhi

with his spinning wheel. The card was from Mukta. She'd made a picture of two girls walking hand in hand under the *neem* tree out of dried rose, marigold, and jasmine petals and *neem* leaves. There was a short letter with it but she didn't mention anything about her *kaki*. I wondered if she'd simply forgotten to write about her, or if her *kaki* had become sicker.

I displayed Mukta's card on the coffee table. All day long I was like a fluttering butterfly in a spring garden. There was so much to do, but I couldn't settle on one task and kept moving about doing a little bit of everything and much of nothing. Mommy and Pappa finished hanging colorful streamers, making bags of party favors, and preparing snacks.

There were six of us and Mela at the party. We played games and I cut the cake and opened the gifts. All afternoon Mommy and Pappa were nearby and there was no problem. But when we were sitting around that evening Carrie asked, "Asha, does your name mean something like Seema's and Mela's?"

"Yes. *Asha* means 'hope,'" she said.

"Hope!" Carrie said, as if she was taking the meaning in. "And yours, Priya? Does it have a meaning?"

"*Priya* means 'one who is loved,'" Priya said.

"I love the way all your names mean something and that you know their significance."

Nobody said anything for a while. All of us were surprised at Carrie's comments.

Jennifer admired the card Mukta had made. "Is this card from your cousin in India?" she asked.

"No. It's from my friend Mukta. We went to school together."

"She must be good at art," Asha said.

"She embroiders well too," I said. I ran to my room and got the handkerchief Mukta had made.

"What does Mukta mean?" Carrie asked.

Why is she so nosy about names? I thought.

Asha and Priya shrugged their shoulders. They didn't know what Mukta meant. "*Mukt* means 'to be free,' so *Mukta* must mean 'one who is free,'" I said.

"Is she free like a butterfly in the sky?" Mela asked.

Everyone laughed. I tried to laugh with them, but couldn't. Carrie's eyes rested on me and seemed to say, I see what's hidden in your eyes.

A slight shiver went through my spine.

Even though we stayed up late watching movies and eating popcorn, my heart was not in my party. It was one o'clock when we turned the lights off. Soon they were all asleep, or at least so I thought. In the dark I picked up Mukta's card and thought about the time we had sat together on a bench and shared a book. The whole time she was with me I complained about it to Urvashi and

Nalini and the other girls at recess, and now I missed her.

"Do you miss your friend Mukta?" Carrie whispered to me.

In the darkness I couldn't see her face, but her voice was soft.

"Yes, I do. I never wanted to be her friend when I was in India, but now that we're apart I wish I could be her friend. Isn't it strange?"

"No, it isn't."

"Why do you say that?" I asked.

"Because it's the same with me. We move every two years and this is my fourth school. Every time we move I end up missing the people I thought I'd miss the least. They're the ones that keep coming to my mind in my new home. I thought I was the only one this happened to," Carrie said.

"I guess not." The darkness stretched between us and for a while we were quiet. "That day at the park . . . what happened? Suddenly, from that day on why did you stop being mean to me?" I asked.

"It wasn't as sudden as you think. It came slowly. After that day in the cafeteria when you said that my name, Schuler, meant 'pain,' and that I was a pain, I was determined to get back at you and make you miserable. You don't know how I tried and schemed. Then, on the day when I teased you about dandelions, I was feeling better.

I saw you walking home that day. You were almost running, and yet I knew you'd be back the next day, and I'd tease you more. After that I got chicken pox."

"And then?"

"While I was sick I realized how much my parents loved me. Mom, who never could sleep if there was a dirty spoon in the sink, ignored the stack of unwashed dishes and pile of soiled laundry when my fever climbed up. Dad took afternoons off and read me stories. They were so good to me."

"But they're your parents. Of course they were good to you—especially when you were sick."

"You don't understand. Every time we move to a new place Dad stays in his office until late and Mom gets busy wallpapering and buying pillows and curtains for the new home. I always feel that the job and house are more important to them than I am. Every time we move I have stomachaches from being nervous about going to a new school, making new friends. There is no one to talk to."

I couldn't imagine moving from one place to another and changing schools all the time. "I'm sorry," I said. "I never realized how difficult it was for you."

"How could you? I was the one making you miserable, until . . ."

"What made you stop? What happened?"

"While I was sick I had lot of time to think about how I

was going to take my revenge. You were the one I thought about the most while I was sick. When I first started school, I'd watched you so intently that I could remember everything about you as if you were right there in front of me. When I got the card that the class had made, the first thing I did was to see if you'd signed it. And you had. You even wrote a message! I realized that if I moved again after a year or two, you'd be the one I'd be thinking of the most. It made me wonder if you and I could be friends. The thought had never occurred to me."

"But why did you pick on me? I hadn't spoiled anything for you so why were you so mean to me?"

"I guess I was scared."

"You? Scared? I remember that way you walked in the cafeteria, your eyes sweeping over us all. Your hair so pretty and such bounce in your step. You looked fearless."

"I wasn't fearless. I picked on you because I heard your heavy accent and I knew you were an easy target. I was hoping that other kids would join me and make fun of you too."

"Like Danny?"

"And Ria and Jennifer."

"Ria and Jennifer are my friends. How could you think that they'd be mean to me? And how could you pull my hair that day?"

"It was a dare. I was standing with Danny, Sam, and a

couple of other boys when I saw you walking by. I said, 'I bet I can go and touch her braid and she won't even notice.' No one believed me, so I had to prove I was right."

"You didn't touch my braid, you pulled it."

"It all happened so fast."

"If we had those instant replays like in football, then we'd know how it happened," I whispered.

"Then we could watch it from many angles."

I was quiet for a minute. "Forget all the angles," I said.

"Okay," she sighed. "Tell me more about Mukta."

"All my friends and I kept a distance from Mukta. Even though she and I shared a bench for a year, and she was thoughtful and friendly, I never considered her my friend."

"Why not?"

"Because she was different. She had one uniform that she wore all week long. Even at the beginning of the school year she'd come to class with sandals held together with ten nails."

Carrie was quiet. I heard the murmur of the trees as if they were listening too. I continued, "Before I came here Mukta gave me that handkerchief I showed you. When I visited her family I realized how little they had and yet how thoughtful and generous they were."

"The embroidery is so beautiful," Carrie said.

"It is. After I came here I began to understand Mukta and how she must have felt, because I was going through the same thing, trying to fit in with everyone."

"I can imagine that. Whenever I change schools I get so scared that I try to . . ." she trailed off.

"Thanks for inviting me," she said, her voice heavy, but soft.

"I'm glad you came," I replied, and I realized I meant it.

We were the last two to get up the next morning.

twelve

After my birthday I had a friend in my class. The rest of
the school year moved fast and then came summer vacation. I went to a public library and enrolled in a reading
program. Reading was fun, but what I was really looking
forward to was my first Fourth of July celebration for which
I wanted to wear something red-white-and-blue. I asked
Mommy if I could buy a new T-shirt with an American flag,
and she agreed. Before we had time to go shopping, on
the morning of July first, the phone rang at five o'clock,
shaking us all out of sleep. It was Kaka. It was late afternoon in India. Dadima had had a stroke earlier that day
and she was in the hospital.

"Is Dadima going to be all right?" I asked, battling my
tears.

"I think so," Mommy said, looking at Pappa. He sat there as if someone had hit him with a can of chickpeas.

"Suman, you must go as soon as possible," Mommy said to him.

"What about the three of you? Mother would want to see all of us, not just me."

"If we can get the tickets we can all go; otherwise you must go alone," Mommy said.

When Mommy talked to Grandma Milan she said, "Don't worry about a thing here. I'll take care of the house as well as the garden."

The next day we were on a flight to India. In the plane I thought about how suddenly everything had changed. Before the phone call I was worried about what I was going to wear on the Fourth of July, and now I was worried about Dadima. The clothes weren't important now. I remembered Dadima explaining a Sanskrit verse she used to sing: "Life is like a flow of water, constantly moving and changing its course. One minute it is flowing smoothly and steadily, and no sooner do you feel in charge of it than the little stones drop in, making splashes and ripples whose heads grow larger and larger." I didn't want the head of this trouble to get any larger.

When I was four I used to tell Dadima, "When I get big, you'll get small and then I'll take care of you." I was frightened now. I prayed, "Please God, let me keep my promise; give me a chance to hold Dadima's hand, rub her forehead, tell her stories, make her laugh, comb her hair, fold her saris, and let her win all the card games. Don't let her slip away before I have the chance to do something."

The monsoon had begun in Mumbai. As soon as we got off the plane I could taste the Arabian Sea, moist and salty. In the customs area the overhead fans whirled furiously. The sounds of familiar languages, the hustle-bustle of porters, and the tinkling of bangles whorled tingles down my limbs.

We reached muggy Vishanagar at eight in the morning. Raju ran across the garden and opened the front gate. The garden was lush after the first rains. I hugged Raju and then Dadaji, Kaki, and Uma, and then Raju again. We were all hugging and crying and talking at the same time. Kaka was at the hospital with Dadima.

"Can we go see Dadima right now?" I asked.

"As soon as you get ready," Mommy said.

"And eat breakfast," Kaki said.

"I'm not hungry. I'm ready to go."

In the rickshaw I sat with Dadaji. Up and down it went on the pothole-covered roads. With one hand I clutched the rail and with the other I clasped Dadaji's arm.

As soon as we entered the hospital I was overcome by the smell of rubbing alcohol. I remembered the smell because Pappa used rubbing alcohol in his lab to disinfect the countertops. In the general ward I saw patients lined up in rows of beds and I thought of Mukta's *kaki*. Before I entered Dadima's room I stopped, took a deep breath, and pulled a smile on my face. When I saw Dadima, so frail and with an IV in her arm, my courage failed. As soon as she saw us her eyes gleamed like the quartz that we used to collect when we were little.

I took her hand in mine, but my words turned to mush in my throat.

Mela stood by the door and wouldn't come in.

"*Aav*, come, Mela," Dadima said. Pappa picked her up and brought her close.

"Do you know who this is?" I asked.

"Daddy's ma, that's Daddyma," she said. We all laughed.

After a while Dadima whispered, "Your skin is lighter, Seema; I suppose you aren't in the sun much in the winter."

"I'm much darker now than I was in the winter. In the winter, it's the sun, not me, that isn't out much. And even when it is, the days are so short that by the time I come home from school the day is done."

"And now in the monsoon the days are longer?"

"There's no monsoon there. It can rain any time. In winter when it's very cold, it snows. Right now the days are very long and it doesn't get dark until nine-thirty."

148

Dadima closed her eyes. She was tired and we quietly slipped out of her room.

I'd seen Dadima and she'd seen me and I'd held her hands. My prayers had been answered, but now I wanted more. I prayed that she would get better and come home.

While we were in the hospital it had rained, and when we came home the mugginess of the morning had disappeared. At lunch Kaka said, "Seema, you must be fluent in English now. While you're here I want you to speak to Raju only in English. He needs the practice."

I glanced at Raju. He didn't say a word, but I noticed that he'd stopped eating. There was a pile of rice and a bowl of dal that he didn't finish.

After lunch Raju and I went to the garden. My eyes feasted on the salmon blooms of woody liana and the magenta blooms of bougainvillea and the rain-polished leaves of the mango tree. The swings were wet and the raindrops sparkled on the roses. Everything was fresh, new and familiar. And then I saw it. I saw a vine covering the bamboo trellis with elliptical leaves dotted with flowers. As I walked toward it, its sweet fragrance filled me completely. "Jasmine? Is this an angel-wing jasmine?" I squealed.

"Yes. Do you like it?" Raju asked.

I stood there admiring the white blooms as delicate as snowflakes.

"We never had an angel-wing jasmine in the garden before. Who planted this?"

"I did. Remember the surprise I told you about? This is it."

"But why didn't you tell me?"

"Because I wanted you to see your jasmine for yourself."

"Is it mine?"

"It is," Raju said. "After you left, Dadaji took me to the nursery on a Rakshabandhan day and asked me to pick out a plant that I could take care of. That way when you came back I'd have a gift for you."

I picked a flower with a raindrop quivering in the center of its seven petals. I touched its petals with my lips. "Oh, Raju, jasmine doesn't grow in Iowa."

"That's why this one is yours. If you stay here, you can enjoy your jasmine everyday."

"I can't, Raju. I have to go back. Remember the picture of the blue flower I mailed you?"

"Yes, I remember," he said.

"It's called hyacinth, but when I first saw it I called it blue jasmine."

"Why did you call it blue jasmine?"

"Because its scent reminded me of jasmine. I have to go back where the blue hyacinths bloom."

He walked to the swing, wiped it with his handkerchief,

and sat down. I sat down, too, and we watched the sky turn from light to dark and then from dark to light again. The monsoon sky and my mood shared the same hue.

"This is the place I missed so much. This is the place I dreamed of the most," I said, looking once around the garden.

"I'd have missed people more than the garden. I, for sure, would've missed you the most," Raju said, turning his face away.

"You know what I mean . . . I'm sorry, Raju. . . ."

He turned back and laughed. "Don't you realize that I'm teasing? No one teases you in America, so I suppose you're out of practice."

I stared at him. "I'm sure that in the past year no one has played tricks on you, so you'll have to be careful, too."

"I'm careful and I'm always ready to learn more tricks," he said.

"Except for English, you're ready to learn," I said.

As soon as those words spilled out of my mouth I wished I could mop them up. His face fell a thousand feet and his eyes turned elephant-gray.

"I shouldn't have said that," I said.

"It's not your fault. It's Pappa. Ever since you went to America he's been after me to study hard. He insists that

I talk to him in English, and you know how hard that is, so I've stopped talking to him altogether. And the less we talk the more annoying I am to him."

"I didn't realize that Kaka was so serious about talking in English," I said.

"Oh yes, he is. He is obsessed with English—American English. Without that, he says, I won't succeed."

"Why didn't you write to me about it?" I said.

"How could I have? You had to face so much more than I did. I avoid my pappa as much as I can."

His words pinched my heart the way a tiny stone in a shoe pinches a foot.

I wanted to give Raju the maps I'd brought. He was so upset that I decided to wait a little longer until his anger had melted away. I wanted to show him Vermont and tell him about the fall colors. I wanted to show him where in Wisconsin Jennifer's grandparents lived. I wanted to show him the state of Georgia, where Mrs. Milan had lived for many years. Maybe later he'll be ready to see it all, I thought hopefully.

For the next five days I went to see Dadima in the hospital. Uma and Raju had school, so after they left in the morning I went and sat with Dadima. I wanted to visit Mukta and go to school with Raju one day, but I decided to wait until Dadima was better.

At night I filled up a new clay pot with water. By the

morning the pot had oozed out the heat and cooled and sweetened the water. Early in the morning I picked fragrant pink roses and cannas and arranged them in an old brass pot with long *asopalav* leaves. Pappa made a thermos full of tea for Dadima. In a motor rickshaw, Dadaji and I went to the hospital carrying water, tea, and flowers.

As soon as we got there I helped Dadima with her tea. She was so weak that her hands trembled so I held her cup, tipped it enough for her to take a sip, and then wiped her face. I helped her change into a new sari and put some oil in her hair and then combed it into a bun. When I folded her sari the first time, it came out jumbled up in a ball. I tried again, and slowly I was able to fold it in a perfect rectangle. I read her the news from *Gujarat Samachar*. I hadn't read any Gujarati in the past year so it felt strange to see the Gujarati script, but soon it became natural to read it again. Some days I played cards with her and Dadaji, and she often won. Her mind was as sharp as ever, which made me feel better. I told stories about our past year in America. There were so many things to tell her and Dadaji that three visiting hours went by quickly. Dadima told all the doctors and nurses that took care of her, "My granddaughter, Seema, has traveled halfway around the world to be with me." It made my heart glow like angelwing jasmine.

* * *

One afternoon when Raju came home from school I gave him the two maps. "You remembered to bring them," he said, opening one.

"I bought them the first time I saw them at a bookstore in Iowa City," I said.

" 'Map of North America,' " he said, reading slowly, as if trying to measure the continent with his mind.

"And what is the other one of?" he asked.

"Open it and see," I said.

" 'Iowa City,' " he read.

"My home is right about here," I said.

"Your home is not in Iowa City. It is here in Vishanagar."

"Raju . . ."

"What? How can you go there for a year and make it your home? How can you forget twelve years of your life and all of us? How can you make Iowa City your home when you already have one?"

"You don't understand. . . ."

"I understand perfectly. You're the one having trouble understanding. You said you like that blue flower that blooms only once a year. What about the plumeria, *pari-jat*, and jasmine that have bloomed for you for the past twelve years? How can you forget them?" he said, folding up the map as he stomped away.

I wanted to yell at Raju and tell him how I felt, but when

154

he was upset he spat out his words and then his mouth closed up like a vacuum-sealed bottle.

Later that afternoon Kaka asked, "Why aren't you talking in English with Seema?"

"I don't know," Raju said.

"You don't know what? English? If you don't try, you'll never learn. Look how fluently Mela speaks English, and she's only five."

I looked at Raju. He was silent. I looked at Pappa, and he was silent. I looked at Mommy, and she was silent. It was not right. Kaka wasn't being fair to Raju and no one spoke up. "Kaka, I'm the one who doesn't speak to Raju in English," I said.

His eyes narrowed, crumpling his brows. "Why? Why don't you speak with him in English?"

"Because when I see Raju only Gujarati comes out of my mouth. I've never talked to him in English, and it feels foolish," I said.

"That's an excuse you're making up for him. I am your *kaka* and I know you. For Raju's sake, teach him to speak English. He knows very well how to read and write English. It's the talking he needs to practice. If he doesn't, he'll have problems when he grows up. Talk to him and teach him."

"I will," I said.

* * *

"Pappa has a grand idea to teach me English. Talk to Seema! From now on when Pappa is around I'm not going to talk to you, Seema. I'll be quiet as Dadima's sateen slippers," Raju said, as we sat on the ebony swing on the front veranda.

The black clouds were parting in the sky and the sun shone through. The garden was swathed in a golden light.

"Let's talk in English when we're alone," I suggested.

"I don't want to,"

"Why not?" I asked.

"Why should we? We've always talked in Gujarati."

"It could be fun."

"Maybe you and Pappa should talk in English and leave me in peace," he said, scowling as he stood up.

"Where are you going?" I asked.

"To see a friend who wants to talk in Gujarati."

Before I could stop him he had slipped on his sandals and skipped down the three steps, and was storming through the garden gate.

I sat on the swing and looked over the garden. The golden glow was gone and the dark clouds were threatening again.

thirteen

It was a Saturday when Dadima came home. In the morning Kaki and Mommy drew swastikas with red vermilion powder on the threshold of the house to protect Dadima and our home and to bring good blessings to us all.

"Here, Seema, draw a swastika. You remember how to draw it, don't you?" Kaki asked.

"Yes, I do," I said.

I was relieved when Dadima came home, but I hadn't realized that instead of visiting her in the hospital, now all her visitors would come to our house. Some came every second day, some came every day, and some, like Dadima's sister, Masiba, came twice a day. It was enough people to tire a healthy person, let alone a sick one. Yet

Dadima thrived on the visitors and was getting better all the time.

Raju had been avoiding me, and when people came they made such a fuss over Mela and me that I saw disgust and pain in Raju's eyes. One evening Masiba and her two sons and their wives and four grandchildren came for a visit. We all sat in the back veranda eating spicy lentil-and-rice bread and mango pickles, and drinking buttermilk, and talking and laughing.

"Mela, recite a poem in English for me," Masiba said, smiling her toothless smile.

Frightened, Mela hid behind Kaki's sari. Mela was afraid of Masiba because whenever Masiba got a chance she affectionately pinched Mela's cheeks. Many other visitors did that too, and now Mela's cheeks were red and raw and she didn't want any more cheek-pinching.

"Seema, Mela's shy. You say something," Masiba said.

"But you don't understand English," I said.

"I still like the sound of it when you say it," she said.

As soon as I said my first sentence in English, Raju got up. I glanced at him. He was staring at the sky with eyes as blank as a moonless, starless monsoon sky.

"Where are you escaping to?" Kaka asked Raju.

"Going out," he replied.

"Why? Are you allergic to us?"

Raju glanced at me and in his eyes I saw the anger that

he tried to conceal from Kaka. He sat down quietly, keeping his gaze fixed on the clouds.

After everyone left, Raju complained to Kaki, "Why do so many people come and visit Dadima over and over again? Masiba comes twice a day. We might as well put her bed in Dadima's room."

"Dadima enjoys her sister's visits. If you were sick, wouldn't you want Uma and Seema to be with you?"

"No, I wouldn't," he said.

The next morning I went to the vegetable market with Dadaji. In my shopping bag I carried a scarf that I wanted to give to the farmer with the glinting eyes. When he travels in the winter the scarf will keep him warm, I thought. It was very early in the morning and some farmers were still arranging their nine-sided okra and the elephant ear—shaped *alvi* leaves in a pile. I listened for the familiar melodious voice of the farmer, but it was missing. My eyes skimmed over each one of the farmers, but I didn't see the one face I wanted to see.

"Who are you looking for?" Dadaji asked.

"Where is the old farmer with the white turban who used to give me carrots and mangoes to eat?" I asked.

"He passed away last winter. I've been buying vegetables from his son here," Dadaji said. My hand slipped into my shopping bag and I clutched the scarf tightly. The farmer with the white turban was gone and the scarf would never keep him warm. The juggling of the scale and the jingling of the coins made me realize that the farmer's son had weighed the tomatoes and Dadaji had paid him the money. I had to open my bag so he could put the tomatoes in it.

"Here," I said, taking out the scarf and handing it to him.

He looked at Dadaji.

"She bought it for your father. Now you take it," Dadaji said.

The farmer put his balance down, took the scarf with both his hands, and touched it to his head. "This will give me good luck for the rest of my life," he said. His eyes glinted just as the old farmer's had. I wondered if the glint of his father's gaze shone in his son's eyes, or if all farmers' eyes glint because they are filled with sunrays.

As we walked home I asked Dadaji, "Why didn't you write me about the old farmer dying?"

He took my arm in his. "I didn't think it was important. But it was. I should have written to you," he said.

"I've made spaghetti for you," I told Uma and Raju when they got home from school the next day.

"I don't think I'll like your spugti," Raju said.

"Can I eat your share then, Raju?" Uma teased.

Raju grunted.

"I'm starving. Let's eat," Uma said.

Raju loved tomatoes, and the sauce was thick and red. When I warmed it up and poured it over the spaghetti, he couldn't resist. "What are those spices?" he asked.

"Basil and oregano. I brought spices and spaghetti from America."

"How do you eat such long, slippery, skinny things?"

"Like this," I said, twirling it on a fork as Grandma Milan had taught me.

"Thanks for making such a good thing to eat," Raju said as he got up from the table. He avoided looking at me.

"It's called spaghetti," I said.

"Whatever. I don't care to learn its name," he said.

"What's your problem? Why are you so mean?"

"You think I'm mean? I'm not the one telling stories about America to everyone who comes to see Dadima. I'm not the one who talks in American English to impress people. I have an idea! Why don't you make a recording of your stories, so after you leave we can play them over and over again?"

"Do you think I like all this fuss-muss over us? If you think I talk American English, you're wrong. Come to my school and they'll tell you all about my Indian accent. Isn't it great that in America I have an Indian accent and in India I have an American one? I came here to see Dadima. I missed everyone and everything so much, but now I see that I was foolish to think that I could ever come back. I wish I'd never come. . . ." There was so much I wanted to spill out, but the words got strangled in my throat.

I walked out into the garden. Raju followed me.

After a few seconds he said, "I'm sorry for getting mad. Since the day you left I've been waiting for you to come back. I thought that when you came back everything would be the way it used to be. Now I know that it isn't possible."

"No, it isn't," I said.

Raju gave me a small smile. On the lawn I traced a flower with my finger.

"Seema, how did you learn to speak English so well?" he asked.

"Once you *have* to talk in English, it becomes natural to talk and think in English."

"If I talk to you in English, will I learn?"

"Yes. It's not hard. Once I started doing it I realized that just as I'd had to string words together to speak Gujarati I had to string words together to speak English."

"I can string words."

"Let's string them in English," I said.

* * *

When Raju was doing his homework that evening, Mommy and I went to the market. I wanted to go to Mukta's house, but I didn't want to tell anyone except Mommy and Pappa. I was afraid that if Raju knew I was going to visit Mukta he would call her stinky and upset me. I knew it was wrong for him to be so nasty to her, but the two of us were having enough problems without my bringing Mukta into it.

That evening the market was more crowded than I'd remembered. Mommy and I hurried to Mukta's shop, but it was closed. The metal door had a big brass lock on it.

"Where do you think Mukta's family went?" I asked.

"I wonder if someone knows," she said, looking around.

The tailor from the shop next door came out, "Are you looking for the Shanti Ganthiawala family?" he asked.

"Yes," we said.

"They have all gone to Ambaji for a pilgrimage."

"Is everyone in the family all right?" I asked.

"Yes, why?" he said. "Did you want to order food for a party? They're going to be back in three days and I can take your order."

I glanced at Mommy. Like me, she realized that the tailor was puzzled. He must've wondered, How can a lady carrying an expensive purse and her daughter wearing foreign-made clothes have anything to do with Shanti

Ganthiawala? That's why he assumed we wanted to order food.

"We're not here to order food," Mommy said.

"Can you please tell Mukta that her friend Seema is here from America?" I said.

"I will tell Mukta as soon as she comes back," he said. Then he turned to Mommy and said, "I sew very good clothes. If you need anything done, sari blouses, petticoats, dresses for your daughter, I make them all in the latest fashions."

"Right now I don't need anything stitched," Mommy said.

He handed her a piece of paper with his name and said, "People take my clothes to America, England, Hong Kong, Singapore, everywhere. I take express orders and get them ready in a day. Unlike other tailors, I won't make you come again and again. I'll even deliver it to your house."

"If I need something, I'll stop by," Mommy said, and we walked toward the vegetable market.

I was disappointed that Mukta wasn't home. "Mom, how far away is Ambaji?" I asked.

"About eight hours from here. Why?"

"I was thinking of how much it might cost to go there."

"Many times people go because they have made a *manta*, a special request that they have asked and prayed for. When their wish is granted, they make a pilgrimage," she said.

"Maybe Mukta's *kaki* is better. I'm sure that's what they asked for and got. Otherwise why would they close the shop and go? It would be every expensive for them to do that. Don't you think?"

"It makes sense," she said. "But there could be other reasons too."

"I don't think so," I said. "I want to come back in three days to see if Mukta is back."

"We will," Mommy promised.

As Dadima got better she began to move around the house a little. Her eyes left nothing undiscovered. "Zeeno," she said, looking toward our servant. "There's a spiderweb in this corner, and the windows are so dusty that we might as well paint them black."

"I'm going to the market this morning, so I'll be sure to bring some paint for the windows," Zeeno replied.

"Looks like your tongue has loosened up while I've been in the hospital," Dadima said.

Zeeno smiled and began cleaning the spiderwebs off the walls.

Dadima looked at Kaki and said, "If we can't eat all the fruit that people have brought, then give it to the poor outside the temple."

"If the people who gave you the fruit baskets find out you're giving them away, their brows will wrinkle."

"Once they give me a gift, what business is it of theirs what I do with it? We'll eat what we can and the rest must go where it can do some good. Let's give some of it to the poor to relieve their hunger."

"I'll go to temple today," Kaki said.

Dadima turned to me. "Seema, come and sit by me and tell me about your Grandma Milan."

"I told you everything, three times over," I said.

"Tell me again. Don't you know that the older we get the younger we become? Like Mela, I need to hear stories again and again to remember them."

So I told her again about Grandma Milan.

In the evening Kaki, Zeeno, and I went to the temple with the extra papayas, pomegranates, bananas, and guavas. There were so many poor people lined up outside the temple that in a few minutes our baskets were empty. I realized that in Iowa City I'd rarely seen a beggar.

The next day Raju said, "Why don't you come to school tomorrow?"

"I'll come next week," I said.

"Why next week? Urvashi, Nalini, all of them have been asking for you," he said.

I wanted to tell him that they could have come to our house to see me. Instead I said, "I'll come Monday, I promise."

Again on Saturday evening I went to see Mukta, but the store was locked and even the tailor's shop was closed, so I couldn't ask him about them. On Sunday we were invited to spend the day at Masiba's house.

The next morning I went to school with Raju. Nalini and Urvashi came running to me, and before I knew it there were six of my old classmates surrounding me.

"Sit by us," Nalini said.

"No," Raju said. "She's going to sit with me."

"You're with Seema all the time. Let her sit with us."

Raju considered. "I suppose Seema can sit by anyone she wants to."

With five minutes left before the bell, I looked around and saw Mukta hurrying through the front gate.

Nalini saw her, too, and made a face, saying, "Maybe Seema wants to sit by her friend Mukta. Remember they shared a desk in fifth grade?"

"Yes, maybe she should sit by her. Wouldn't that be funny?" said Urvashi.

"Do you want to?" asked Nalini, expecting me to twist my face.

"For the first period I'll sit by Mukta," I said.

"Don't joke now. It's not April Fool's Day," Urvashi said.

By now Mukta was only ten feet away. "Seema, is that you?" She walked two steps and stopped. All the eyes were on her and they were not all friendly.

"Mukta," I said, breaking away from the crowd. "I came to your house twice, but you weren't there."

"We got back late last night. I wasn't going to come to school today, but when I woke up I felt I had to come, and now I know why!"

Mukta and I walked toward the class. I was so busy talking to her that I forgot what the other girls were doing. Raju was walking next to me. "I'm going to sit by Mukta for the first class, and for the next class, I'll sit by you," I told him.

"That's fine," he said.

Once I had sat down, I looked around. There were fifty-five kids in the class, all with the same dark heads. The boys had short hair and the girls all wore braids. All the boys looked the same from the back and all the girls looked the same from the back. I realized that in Iowa City I'd learned to recognize my classmates from the color and style of their hair.

I was afraid that if the teacher asked me a question I'd forget to stand up while answering it. In the first period the teacher asked me to read aloud from a Gujarati play. As I stood up to read, I felt glad that I'd read to Dadima before, so that my tongue rolled out the words as smoothly as my eyes floated over them.

In the class, Mukta and I couldn't talk much, but I did get a chance to ask her how her *kaki* was. She was better, but she was still at the sanitarium in the dry region of Jitheri. We both wanted to tell each other many things, so we decided to spend a day together before I left. I didn't want to invite her to our house. All those years it had been my home, but now I felt that it was more Raju's home than mine. Mukta didn't want me to come to her house, because there was no privacy for us, and she was afraid that the smoke from the frying in their shop might make me sick. When Raju and I walked home, we passed the acacia. Because of all the rain, ferny leaves covered the entire tree. It reminded me of spring in Iowa.

That Friday I went to spend the day with Mukta. Mommy took me to the market at ten and said she'd pick me up at four. The tailor's shop was busy, and as soon as we were close enough he emerged with a dress for a young girl. The dress was red with light blue smocking on the front.

"Look at this, sister," he said to Mommy. "This is my work. All mine."

Mommy took the dress in her hands and I touched the cotton sateen. It was soft, with a glossy finish, and the blue smocking was done in matte thread. It reminded me of the pictures we sent to be developed. It always asked on the envelope if you wanted a glossy or matte finish. On the dress the tailor had combined both beautifully.

Mommy turned it around in her hand and said, "What do you think, Seema?"

Before I could answer, the tailor said, "I know you have no use for this little dress. This is to show you my work. I can make one for her."

"Get one for Mela," I whispered to Mommy.

"How much?" she asked.

"Two hundred rupees. This belongs to a client, though, and I have to deliver it this afternoon, but I can make you one in four hours," he said.

"Make me one exactly the same," she said.

The tailor nodded happily and returned to his shop.

"See you in a few hours," Mommy said to me.

Before I could climb the steps to Mukta's shop, she came out.

Mukta and I were going to the temple. There was a big courtyard in the temple, and we decided that we'd spend a day under the shade of the *neem* tree there, and if it rained we could always go into the temple. No sooner had we walked past three shops than we passed two boys carrying three baskets of flowers. The smell filled the air. Mukta stopped and looked back.

"Are they going to your house?" I asked.

"Yes. But I thought we weren't going to have flowers today."

"Do you want to go back and find out what's happening?"

She hesitated.

"Let's check," I said.

We approached the open area behind Mukta's house where the baskets filled with roses·and marigolds were delivered by the boys. Mukta looked at the flowers, and glanced at her mother.

"Go," her mother said. "You've made plans with Seema."

"But this is a special order. We'll get so much money for it," Mukta said.

"I'll get them done."

"How? That's too much work for you, and if the tailor's wife helps you, we won't make much money."

I noticed the spools of thread and needles in a plastic box, and I realized that they made their garlands outside. If we didn't have to be in a dark room all day I didn't mind talking to her right there. "Why don't we sit here and talk while you make garlands?" I said.

"Maybe I can do some and then we can go out," Mukta said.

Mukta's fingers moved as fast as Asha's fingers when she played the piano. They both had a lot of practice. "Can I try?" I asked.

One flower after another slid down the thread until it turned into a garland. While I made one garland, Mukta made twelve.

"Are schools different in America?" Mukta said.

"In a way they are and in a way they're not. In the beginning it was difficult to face other students who spoke satin-smooth English that I didn't understand. When I saw their skin, eyes, and hair so different from mine, I realized I was far from my home. But I had my friends Jennifer and Ria to help me. My teacher, Ms. Wilson, was kind and patient with me, and slowly, as I began to understand English, I felt comfortable."

"So with each passing day it became easier and easier?"

I thought of the cold winter and Carrie. "It was like a *saap-sidi*, a chutes-and-ladders game. Many days when I did well in school and talked to my friends, I felt that I'd climbed a ladder, but then there were days when I slid down the chutes."

I told Mukta about winter and snow, about my struggle with English and all the things I had done wrong, including putting dandelions in my hair.

"Sometimes I'm jealous of Mela," I said.

"Why?"

"Because Mela is only five. She speaks English without an accent. She has hardly any memory of India to haunt her. She'll start kindergarten next year and I know she'll be so happy. I wish I could be like her, with no yearning and, and . . ." I trailed off.

"And complete belonging?" Mukta said, laying a rose garland she'd just finished in the basket.

"Yes. That's it."

She didn't reply. She began a new garland of marigolds. I realized that she would never understand how it was to go to a foreign country. She was where she'd always been. After a few minutes Mukta said, "You get twice as long a vacation as I do. I wish I had that."

"Raju wishes the same. Everyone wants a long vacation. No one wants long school and all the work that goes with it," I said.

Mukta drew a deep breath. "It's different for me. If I had a longer vacation I could work and make money and help my family. Around here none of the girls my age are in school. The tailor's girl only finished fourth grade and now she helps sew and makes money. Their son is in eighth grade, and they're talking about not sending him to school anymore."

"You're smart. You're different from all those girls who don't study after fifth grade," I said.

"Seema, all those girls are not dumb. They don't study because they don't have money."

"You're right. You said your tuition was paid by someone last year. What about this year?" I said.

"My tuition has been paid until I graduate from high school. That's what our principal told Mommy, so I'll continue school, but it worries me."

"If your fees are paid, what's there to worry about?"

"Plenty. I'm thirteen. I should be making money and helping my family. In our community the girls get married by the time they're sixteen or so, and if I work for the next few years I can make money and save some for my wedding. With Kaki's sickness we've used up all our money, including Mommy's two gold bangles."

"You're not like the girls who get married at sixteen. You have to go to school," I said.

"What do you mean I'm not like a girl who gets married at sixteen? Going to school doesn't make me like you, or Urvashi, or Nalini. Your parents are educated; they have money. You don't have to worry about food, and you don't have to share a room with six other people. When holidays come and everyone talks about going on vacations, I cringe. We've no place to go. Going to Ambaji was our first trip. Kaki got better, but she needs to stay in the sanitarium for three more months."

"Oh, Mukta!"

"Seema," she whispered, "ever since I can remember I've dreamed of being like all of you at school. Do you know that I've never bought a snow cone in the summer or salted peanuts from a vendor? The only time I have a lollipop or a candy is when someone brings it to school as a treat to share, and I am ashamed to eat it, because I've never brought any for anyone else. Every birthday I've wished that the next birthday I could take sweets for the class. Now that I'm old enough I know how impossible it is."

My heart was stunned into silence. I stared at the peeling paint on the outside wall of Mukta's house. The door was open and I peered inside, but it was so dark that I saw nothing but a gaping hole. I thought of the handkerchief that Mukta had given me. It was a thousand times more precious now. I wondered how she'd bought it.

"How did you buy the material and the embroidery threads for the handkerchief you made me?" I asked.

"I didn't buy it. It's good to have a tailor living next door. We always barter with our neighbors. The tailor sews our clothes for free and gives us scraps of material and we give him snacks in return. For your handkerchief he took a white piece of muslin and finished the edging and then gave me thread to embroider it. Do you still have it?"

"Yes, I do."

Mukta smiled. "You're making the garlands really fast now," she said.

"Yes, I am," I said, realizing I was stringing them faster than when I'd started. It takes practice to string together both flowers and words.

The next few days passed quickly. For a week we went to see my other grandparents, Nanima and Nanaji, and when we came back I saw Mukta one last time.

"Seema, I was thinking about you. I wanted to see you, but I thought you might be busy with your family," Mukta said.

"I will be this evening. I came to give you this," I said, giving her a gift.

"What's in it?" she said as she carefully unwrapped the package. I was anxious for her to rip it open.

When she saw the set of mechanical pencils and bundle of refills her face brightened in a smile that reminded me of her mother's smile. "I . . . these are too beautiful for me. I . . . I don't think I'll ever want to use them."

"I brought them for you to use, not to save," I said.

"But what if I lose or break one?" she said, more to herself than to me.

"Then I'll bring another set next time," I said.

"*Na, na,*" she said, grabbing my hand. "That's not what I meant. I'll use it carefully. You shouldn't buy me such an expensive gift again."

I wanted to tell her it was nothing compared to the handkerchief she'd made for me. Instead I said, "I'm so glad you like it."

Then I gave her two boxes of crayons and two packets of colorful construction paper for her sister and cousin. "I have something for you, too," she said.

She gave me a gift wrapped in a banana leaf. As I was

opening it, I thought that it might be the handkerchiefs that she said she was going to make me. If they were the handkerchiefs, I was afraid that they'd be stained by the banana leaf and ruined. But once I opened the leaf I saw that the real gift was still hidden inside layers of newspaper. Even though she'd made the same pattern on these handkerchiefs as the one she'd sewn before, her new work was finer.

"Thank you," I said.

"Have you used the one I gave you before?"

"I . . . I really haven't," I said.

"Promise me that you'll use it," she said.

"I will. But I'll put them on my dresser rather than use them as a handkerchief."

"Why?"

"Otherwise they'll be ruined," I said.

"Seema, I can make you more."

"I know. Still . . ."

"Now you know why I don't want to use the pencils you gave me."

"Yes," I said.

Mukta walked back with me for a couple of blocks, and when we said *avaje*, "come back," to each other, I felt calm. Even if she never came to America, I knew I was taking her back with me. As long as I remembered her, she was with me. I clutched the banana-leaf package, the most beautiful package I'd ever received.

fourteen

Raju and I had been practicing English when the two of us were alone. I taught him the phrases, "You're pulling my leg," and "It's as easy as pie," and my favorite, "You left the barn door open." The last one, I was sure, Kaka wouldn't know.

The day before leaving, as we sat down to eat our meal together, Raju and I began talking in English. Kaka was so astonished that his spoonful of *dal* froze in midair.

"So you did teach him English," he said to me.

"I didn't teach him. He knew it. All he had to do was to learn to string his words together and say them out loud."

"She did teach you, didn't she?" he asked Raju.

"Of course she did. She's pulling your leg," Raju said.

"What?" Kaka asked.

"Pappa, it was as easy as pie," Raju said, his eyes twinkling.

"Do you two understand what Raju is talking about?" Kaka asked Mommy and Pappa.

"Yes, we do," Mommy said.

"It's time for *you* to learn some English," Dadima said to Kaka.

"You left the barn door open with that one, Pappa," Raju teased.

Kaka shook his head and laughed.

That night when I summoned sleep, it wouldn't come. I felt very tired and very awake at the same time. I thought about our return the next day. It felt different from the first time we'd left. This time I was going back to a place where I knew the names of the trees, and patterns of their growth. I was familiar with Iowa City, its streets, grocery stores, parks, and people. Most important, I was not just leaving the people I loved, I was also going back to people I loved. With that last thought, my heart became lighter and my eyes became heavy with sleep.

Tears streamed down my cheeks as I waved to Raju. I held on to Pappa's hand tightly. Once we were on the plane, my heart thumped wildly.

It was two o'clock at night when the plane took off.

Mela was asleep, and soon Pappa and Mommy were too. Meanwhile, I felt like a bat stirring while the world slept.

I must have dozed off, because when I opened the window shade I was bombarded by sunlight. Soon, the flight attendant came around and handed me a warm towel. The smell of cologne rose from the towel as I wiped my face, and the last of the sleep disappeared from my eyes. I kept the warm towel on my face until it cooled off completely. People were chatting now and their voices filled the air. I heard the sound of their talk and caught a word here and there.

Two hours before we reached Chicago, Pappa asked, "Seema, are you glad that we took this trip?"

"Yes. At first I wanted everything to be the same," I said, "but everyone has changed. Dadaji seemed frail. It was as if Dadima's stroke made Dadaji's limbs weak. Kaka demanded more from Raju than he ever did before."

"Yes. You're right," he said. "What else did you find different?"

"That I really like Mukta, and that I'm glad she can finish high school. She told me that someone had paid her tuition."

"I know," he said.

"You know? How did you know?"

"Kaka paid it."

"Kaka? *My kaka*?" I was astonished.

"Yes, Seema. Do you find that hard to believe?"

"No . . . yes . . . I mean, I didn't think Kaka would ever do something like that."

"You don't know all there is to know about your *kaka*. He's like a coconut, tough on the outside, sweet on the inside."

I shook my head in disbelief. I couldn't believe we were talking about the same man.

"When we were young, Kaka never paid attention in school," Pappa said. "And now he realizes that if he had, he might have had more opportunities open up to him."

"Like you?" I asked.

"Yes. He hopes Mukta finishes high school, and maybe more," he said.

"Is that also why he insists that Raju study so hard?"

"Yes."

I thought about this for a while. "Do you think they think I've changed?" I asked Pappa.

"Probably," he said.

"I think they did, and I have. I wonder how things would be if we'd never gone to America?"

"Do you wish you hadn't?"

"Oh, no. If we hadn't gone, I wouldn't have met Jennifer, Ria, and all my other friends. I can't imagine how it would be without ever seeing snow, without smelling blue hyacinths filled with the fragrance of jasmine, without gathering colorful leaves and walking in the warm fall sunshine. I'm glad we went to India, but I'm glad we're going back to Iowa City."

"Next time we visit, you may find even more changes," he said.

A quiver made a squiggle through my heart. Something could happen to Dadima or Dadaji. Mukta might have to start working, and she might have a difficult time finishing school, I thought.

"Yes, I may find other changes. But I'm ready for whatever may come along, because I've changed, and I'll keep changing," I said, looking outside. The plane had climbed above one more layer of clouds and now the sun was bright.

"One thing is about to change," he said.

"What's that?"

"Vacation! Your school is starting the day after tomorrow."

"That's one change that I could have done without," I laughed.

Shutting my eyes I imagined the next few days. We were moving from a big house with a garden into a small apartment, and I wondered how Mommy would like that. I thought about starting seventh grade and Mela starting kindergarten.

I remembered how last year when I came to Iowa City

I had no idea what I was going to see and who I was going to meet. This time, I could picture the snow falling on my dark hair, I could hear Grandma Milan calling me "sweet pea," and I could almost smell the jasmine-like scent of the blue hyacinths.

We'd arrived in Iowa City only a year earlier, but the new surroundings and new experiences made me feel like it had happened a long time ago. I'd seen a world I didn't know existed, and I'd learned much from it. Perhaps the more you learn about the world, I thought, the more you learn about yourself.

It had been less than a day since I left India, and I already missed sitting with Raju on the swing and the sparkle of Dadima's eyes when I talked to her about America. I missed my angel-wing jasmine with a raindrop nestled in the middle of its seven petals.

A sharp pain swirled up from my heart. I opened my eyes and looked out the window. We were still very high in the sky, and I couldn't see any land. Now the sun was overhead, but the wing of the plane, as if it were a trampoline for sunbeams, shone and sparkled.

Like an airplane attached to two shimmering wings, I was attached to two precious homes.

glossary of terms and expressions

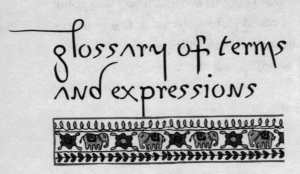

badam: almond

bandhani sari: *bandhani* means "tie-dye." Bandhani saris have vibrant colors and unique patterns.

bapre: "Oh, my goodness!"

bhai: brother

brinjal: eggplant

chakerdi: small spinning ground fireworks

crore: 100 *lakhs*; the number 10 million

dadaji: grandpa

dadima: grandma

Diwali: the Hindu Festival of Lights; a family-oriented feast, with both religious and secular sides, which has cultural importance and feeling somewhat comparable to that of Christmas in the United States

diya: a small clay oil lamp lit outdoors on Diwali

fafda: spicy fried noodles

fatak: the sound of being slapped

ghugra: a special sweet made of cream of wheat, cardamom, and raisins that Gujaratis make at Diwali

Gujarati: the language of Gujarat, a region in northwestern
India, spoken by about 44 million people worldwide

kaka: uncle

kaki: aunt

kem: why

khadi sari: a sari made from rough, homespun white
cotton

lakh: the number 100,000

mashakari: fun, as in making fun of someone

namaste: a greeting or farewell gesture with hands folded
in front of the chest

nanaji: grandpa

nanima: grandma

neem: a majestic, fragrant tree whose oil has many medicinal uses

O, bhaisab!: "Oh, brother!" (literally "Oh, honorable
brother!")

om: a sacred sound, used in chanting and meditation and,
in written form, considered a symbol of good luck

parijat: a tropical shrub with fragrant white flowers and
orange stems, which blooms during the monsoon

Rakshabandhan: a festival that traditionally celebrates

brotherly duty and sisterly love, during which women
of all ages tie specially made threads or cloth bracelets
called *rakhi*s around their brothers' wrists to ensure
their welfare and protection from evil

rotli: also known as *roti*; a thin, whole-wheat bread
cooked on a stove

satyagraha: "truth force," "soul force"; the name given
by Indian nationalist leader Mahatma Gandhi to nonviolent political resistance

shiro: a saffron-flavored pudding made from toasted
semolina and milk

shloka: a verse from a longer Hindu prayer *(stotra)* in the
ancient Sanskrit language; *shloka*s are sung as prayers
or sometimes as lullabies

swastika: a symmetrical cross with bent arms; in India, the
swastika is an ancient symbol of good fortune, which
may originally have represented the sun. The German
Nazi party adopted a form of the swastika as its
symbol in the 1920s.

tal-sankali: a candy made from sesame seeds and sugar

Uttarayan: Kite Flying Day, an Indian holiday, on January
14, that celebrates the sun's return to the Northern
Hemisphere, when children engage in contests using
kites whose strings are treated with powdered glass
to make them strong.